Anonymous

The Amulet

A Tale of Spanish California

Anonymous

The Amulet
A Tale of Spanish California

ISBN/EAN: 9783337024215

Printed in Europe, USA, Canada, Australia, Japan

Cover: Foto ©Andreas Hilbeck / pixelio.de

More available books at **www.hansebooks.com**

THE AMULET:

A TALE OF SPANISH CALIFORNIA.

LONDON:

LONGMANS, GREEN, AND CO.

1865.

PREFACE.

THE accompanying Tale makes no claim to the character of an elaborate work of fiction. It was compiled rather than written, during short intervals of leisure, from a variety of memoranda and notes relating to the people, social habits, occupations, sports, and physical characteristics of the lower part of Alta-California.

In the year 1852 this was a thinly-populated country, solely devoted to the ráising of cattle and horses. The proprietors of the soil were mostly native Californians of Spanish or Mexican descent, their labourers and herdsmen being either half-castes or of pure Indian blood.

From the 37th parallel of latitude southwards, the social aspect of the country was unchanged by its cession to the United States. The tide of enterprise, and the new race of Anglo-Americans, which entered the country by the harbour of San Francisco, set northwards towards the gold region; only a few gentlemen settling around San José, or on the southern shores of the great bay.

The wealth of the great Ranchéros (or cattle-graziers) was increased ten-fold, owing to the demand for cattle in the now populous gold region of the north. This, however, was in some measure balanced by a heavy land-tax imposed by the United States Government.

The sketches of social life, of physical geography and scenery, as well as any notices of the vegetable or animal inhabitants of the country, are based on personal observation, and may be confirmed by reference to the latter part of Mr. Froebel s valuable work on ' Central America, Mexico, and the Far West of the United States.'

CONTENTS.

—◦◦◦—

CHAPTER VIII.

CHAPTER IX.

CHAPTER X.

CHAPTER XI.

CHAPTER XII.

CHAPTER XIII.

CHAPTER XIV.

CHAPTER XV.

CHAPTER XVI.

CHAPTER XVII.

THE AMULET.

CHAPTER I.

LOS OJITOS (THE LITTLE SPRINGS).

IN the lower part of Alta California, between the Sierra de Las Salinas and the sea-shore, lies a pleasant tract of land. Its name is pronounced, Anglicè, Los O'hetos, the o's round and sonorous. The little springs, rising near the house, unite, and form a clear perennial stream, which, winding westward for a mile, loses itself in the sea.

This *Rancho* is at the same distance north of the equator as the island of Crete, or the valley of Cashmere; so I will not descant upon its climate. The house is a two-storied building, long and low, with a red-tiled roof and broad overhanging eaves. A double balcony or corridor runs along the front, which looks westward towards the sea. On to these corridors the doors and windows open, and at either end is a cedar staircase.

B

Before the great house, some twelve paces off, stands a well-constructed *ramada*, or house of boughs, about twenty-four feet square, open in front, and supported by smooth pillars of the *palo colorado*. A few low stools are its only furniture. Over a fire in the middle are suspended three iron vessels; and at about two o'clock in the afternoon, the bower is redolent of stewed beef, chilis, tomatas, and what not. In hot weather it serves both for kitchen and *comedor*. You lounge against a pillar with your plate in hand, or sit upon a stool with plate on knees, according to fancy. But I anticipate. A solitary Indian girl tends the pots: otherwise house and bower are tenantless.

Let us follow the babbling stream. It soon leads us to a pretty tableau, and a prettier babble than its own. Four women are kneeling, each at the upper end of a smooth white board, which slopes down from her waist to the pebbles on either margin of the stream. They are washing. First, they dash a gourd of water over the linen, then rub it with soap, then knead it vigorously, and so on; until at last it is tightly twisted and thrown aside into a basket.

The morning is hot, but our lady-washers are under the shelter of a broad canopy which spans the rivulet. Weeping willows grow on either side, and in this spot their long boughs have been interlaced, so as to form a grateful shade.

Two of these ladies are on either side of the brook, which, just here, is narrow and deep, and is bridged over above the bower. Their lithe movements, as they rock to and fro, stoop forward to dip the gourd, or turn round to throw a finished piece into the basket, enable you to see them all four in various positions; and an animated conversation which is going on enables you to hear the modulation of their voices, with the ripple of the current as an under-tone.

They talk volubly, softening the hard consonants, gliding from one to another, but lingering upon the broad vowels, a fair balance of sound, graceful and well poised.

One lady was several years older than the other three. Now and again one of these would call her *Madre*, though one only was her child. The other two were younger sisters of her husband, but had never known a mother. I think either of those girls would have given up a lover at Madre's bidding; yet one must admit that they have a headstrong, un-reasoning way about those matters, as we shall perhaps see before long.

But I do not get on with my sketch. The senior lady has a melancholy face, unrelieved by a loose black dress, which is confined but slightly at the waist with a heavy cord. There is no moroseness, however, about her look, and much play about the mouth when she speaks. Her hair is silky and black, her eyes dark and lustrous.

The two *señoritas* on the other side of the stream resemble each other closely, but the first has hair a

shade lighter than the other. They both have drooping, black-fringed eyelids, pearly teeth, and a com-
plexion clear but brunette. The thick soft hair falls
rather forward on forehead and cheek, but is drawn
back and divided behind the neck, falling down the
back in two broad plaits. A little bright kerchief
round the neck heightens the colour, as you know.
These are Julia and Francesca.

The young lady behind Madre, the one whom they
call 'Nita' and occasionally 'Niña,' is unlike the rest.
If it were not for a frequent loving look, you would
scarcely take her for Madre's child. Her head is
rounder and her face smaller than those of the other
three. Loose masses of chesnut hair, with a golden
tinge flashing through it in her constant movements,
fall about her sweet face and bosom. Ever and anon
she tosses them back, in vain, except to show you the
lilies and roses of her cheek. And as to her lips, we
know there is nothing in art or nature like a pair of
ruby lips with a glimmer of pearls between. Moreover, her eyes are heavenly blue, and she is at this
time just seventeen years of age.

I was obliged to have a *donzella* of seventeen. You
would never have read my story without her; and if
it had been necessary to scour the country far and
near, I must have found her: so now, as she happens
to be *in limine,* let us be content.

On the former evening, two strangers, travel-soiled
and on foot, asked entertainment for the night.
'*Pasen adelante, señores,*' had been the courteous

welcome. So the travellers walked in and laid their burdens aside; the *cigarito* was proffered and smoked: conversation ran on in its former channel, a pastoral one; glanced thence to poesy, to music. Don Mariano (Madre's husband) played the guitar and sang (all Mexicans do); the ladies sang in chorus; Dons Estéban and Alberto, Mariano's younger brothers, sang; Don Guillermo, the big stranger, sang; and the puzzle to the whole party was that he fingered the guitar and sang better than the Señor himself, the pink of *caballéros*, and spoke a purer Castilian than Madre herself, in whose veins ran the bluest blood of Old Castile.

Yet his physique was of the Saxon type, and every now and then he would address his comrade in English. The latter was a surly-looking young man, half proud, half shy, who either was unable or unwilling to join the conversation.

Only when the ladies had retired, and the gentlemen were consuming tobacco in the corridor below, did the host ask his guests whence they came. 'From the northern mines; by way of San Francisco and Monterey.' 'On foot?' [A Ranchéro never walks fifty yards.] 'Yes, on foot.' '*Ca-a-Rramba!* Two hundred leagues a-foot! *Aquellos hombres!*'

Well, the four ladies are washing away with great vigour, as we have said, and holding an animated conversation. What we noticed when listening just now was their sweetness of voice and grace of utterance; but if we were to familiarise ourselves with the language and their rapid way of speaking, we should hear them discussing their new acquaintances.

The manners and speech of Don Guillermo have impressed them favourably, and a certain romantic air about the other stranger, with his short dark curly hair, and sad grey eyes, was more attractive to the ladies than to those astute Dons Estéban and Alberto.

Last evening, and again at the morning chocolate, the señoras noticed that ' Carlo,' as his friend called him, did not eat till they were served, and would wait on them instead of letting them serve him as they would have done. The simple creatures also noticed that his hands were small and delicate, though bronzed by exposure; whereas the large paws of Estéban and Alberto protruded angrily from the tight sleeves of their short Ranchéro jackets.

' *Pero son Yanqués*,' said the Doña Julia, in a dolorous tone : for these new citizens were ill affected to the Great Republic. [A.D. 1852.]

' No, my child,' Madre answered; ' *son Ingléses*, they are Englishmen. The *cabelléro* told your brother this morning. He was attached to the British Legation in Madrid.'

> ' Paz con Inglaterra,
> Y con todo el mundo guerra,' *

shrilled Juanita, tossing back her fulvous locks and looking defiance at Julia. But the latter main-

---

* Peace with England, and war with all the world.

tained a peaceful demeanour, and soaped her linen demurely.

In the meantime a scene of still greater activity is taking place in the *corral*, at a distance of half a league.

The *corral* is an oblong cattle-pen, formed of red-wood stakes, driven deep into the ground. At one end a hundred and twenty cows and as many calves were standing huddled, lowing angrily. At the other end the Dons Estéban and Alberto presided over a large fire, which struggled fitfully against the bright sunlight. Each held a long branding rod, with one end in the fire. The Señor Don Mariano, on a strong roan horse, occupied the middle space, and poised a lasso : near him stood three *vaquéros*, or native herds-men. The Englishmen had been counselled, in plain Spanish, to keep behind the fire, and to look out for squalls : so they stood quietly and watched the performance.

The Señor cast his lasso into the throng : the roan backed, and dragged out a heifer. Then the three *vaquéros* seized the lasso and ran firewards, dragging the heifer across the open space. The cow charged, but Don Mariano engaged her midway, waving his *sombréro*, and making his horse prance and curvet before the furious beast. So the first yearling was branded, loosed, and bounded bellowing back to its angry parent. These manœuvres were repeated, and the clamour increased.

' *Mira estos hombres* !' said Alberto to his brother,

in consternation; for, in defiance of orders, the two strangers moved along under the palisade, approaching the herd; nearer, nearer: the brutes shrink back; Don Guillermo draws the noose of a lasso round a heifer's neck, grasps the tail also, and drags it off, saying to the other, ' Have a care, Carlo !'

' *Quedado!*' shouted Don Mariano from the centre; for in the meanwhile the maternal cow came down upon them furiously; and as Carlo slipped aside, her horn passed through his flannel shirt, above the belt.

'*Ca-a-Rramba!*' exclaimed the horseman: but the simple Carlo, turning, vexed the cow in the rear: and another roar came from the fire as the calf was branded. Then the game grew fast and fiery. Don Mariano and his men, Don Guillermo and his friend, vied with each other which should make the most despatch.

As they returned to the house, Don Alberto made the following remark to Don Estéban: ' *Demonios son estos hombres!*'

Nor was the proof of their energy lost on Mariano Arianas, that keen observer, on the roan horse.

CHAPTER II.

EL DORADO.

What is here?
Gold? Yellow glittering precious gold.

ALL the world's a stage. Having plunged *in medias res*, and introduced the ladies first, according to the laws of arts and manners, let us restore an act, played out some two months since, but in which our two Englishmen sustained the principal parts.

In a small log cabin at the foot of Mount Shasté, two men are sleeping. The last ember has ceased to glow. A cold grey light and a low temperature pervade the place. The latitude is that of Tortosa, Naples, and the Golden Horn : but fourteen thousand feet above the valley, above the climbing groves of oak and cypress, soars the radiant peak of Shasté, crowned with everlasting snow : wherefore it is cold.

One of the sleepers moves, yawns, flings abroad his arms, and then with bent elbow rests his head upon one hand. He is a splendid fellow. You may see it in the dusky light of dawn. Large of limb, and broad of shoulder ; grey-eyed and tawny-haired.

With a look half-quaint, half-sad, he turned to the companion of his woes, and mused, 'My poor Carlo! No wonder it has floored you. Hope deferred for five weary months, and then swept away with such a rude harsh hand. And those pretty brats at home, to whom my legacy should have gone. Ah, well! sighing won't dam a watercourse. How Carlo raged! and now the storm is spent, how dolorously he clings to mother earth!' And down the gorges plunged the river with its ceaseless roar.

William Briggs lifted his gaunt body from the ground, and presently his broad back loomed over a cheerful blaze: but the torrent's roar sounded in his ears like the mocking of a fiend: and Carlo, groaning in his sleep, and clutching at the earth with pallid fingers, smote him with a sense of wretchedness.

For on the former day a calamity had befallen them. Ill brooking the throng of men in populous diggings, where the gold was known to be plentiful, they had moved up the country some months before; packing their tools and blankets, with ammunition and provisions, upon a much-enduring mule, and travelling themselves on foot, carrying each a rifle, for this was the land of the red-deer and the grizzly bear.

Beating up the left bank of the river,* sometimes on its margin, sometimes toiling over rugged cliffs, through which it dashes violently, they 'prospected'

* Rio Sacramento.

as they went along. The river-bed had yielded large quantities of gold in its lower course, and they thought that in some hollow nearer to its source a deposit might be found.

And so it was. They struck upon a crevice in the bed-rock. It ran outwards from the river, and then along, parallel with it. Its jagged ridges were filled and overlaid with a stiff clay, in which the gold was bedded. So they cleared a space of surface earth, a dozen feet in width, and about one hundred and fifty yards in length, 'prospecting' as they reached the clay, which guided them along the crevice. `

Months of severe labour and privation. They built a hut on the mountain slope, toiled and slept, toiled and slept; for the gold-fever was upon them; in their veins coursed the fire, and over them the demon flapped his wings.

Sunday was spared from toil, with bitter but constrained reluctance. Life was more than gold. Their flour was exhausted: the tea had gone. They eked out the ammunition jealously: each charge of powder and ounce of lead representing so much meat. Only on Sunday was a shot fired: then one would take the constant mule, and go up into the mountains to seek the deer: the other would hover about the claim, armed, and ill at ease; for now the gold-fever was spreading, the Indians were on the gold-trail; they were no longer to be trusted. They would lurk round the cutting, and after pelting storms, when the sun glistened on the clay or naked rock, revealing its treasures, would gather round impetuously to seize the glittering grains.

But the two friends resolved that their claim should be sacred, and that if necessary they would guard it with their lives. So it was a weary time for stomach, heart, and brain : and when at last the treasure was within their grasp, when the precious clay, with its untold wealth, was collected in a few small mounds, and a week's careful washing would have set them free, free with the whole world for their home, and a welcome everywhere among the haunts of men ; down had come the rushing torrent, and swept it all away in one wild flood, and left them homeless on the mountain-side.

So the two wanderers sat over their fire, tearing their shred of salted vension, each willing that the other should begin to talk. Most of us know what it is to complete a task, and to feel that we can do no more. So it was with them. They had toiled, endured, suffered. The limit had been reached. The same feeling was uppermost with each, 'Let us go.'

Silently they put their blankets on the patient mule, little else they had to pack, and turned their faces southwards.

*   *   *   *   *

At San Franciso they exchanged their little bag of prospect-gold for coin. It was about a hundred dollars, or less than £20 in all.

Still, Briggs was the possessor or inheritor of £2,000, and knew that he might draw on the firm of Starchie

for part or whole of that sum; but five little sisters
and three tall lads had to be provided for at 'home:'
and William, whose heart was big and strong like his
body, would leave his legacy to who might want it
more, and turn an honest penny for himself.

Starchie senior was an old friend of William's
father. He advised the two adventurers to go still
southwards, and take to farming or to cattle-grazing.
William might buy land, at a dollar and a quarter
per acre, of the State; or he might spend a year
on a Rancho, which was in good working trim, to
get an insight into the system. He gave William an
introduction to one Señor Don Jose Joaquin, &c.;
and the friends started together, modestly, on foot.

But Carlo knew nothing about William's legacy, or
alluring prospects. He cared little about merchant
or hidalgo; for a dull cloud had fallen and closed
around him. Through the darkness he grasped one
hand only, and firmly: and it will be seen hereafter
that it is well to grasp a strong hand and to trust a
true heart.

CHAPTER III.

A CHECK.

TWO or three days had elapsed since the arrival of the two strangers at Los Ojitos. They stood at their bedroom door in the clear moonlight.

' Slow place this, Carlo,' said one.

' Well, I don't know,' was the answer; ' we wanted to see something of Ranchéro-life, and I'm sure the stout hidalgo is awfully civil.'

W. B. You called him ' the fat Don ' a day or two ago.

C. Yes; but that was my country manners. One gets a little polish, living amongst women.

W. B. Hem! Don't you think now, we might move southwards to-morrow ?

C. O, of course, if you like. ' *Teucro duce,*' &c.

But this was said testily. So he of the tawny beard made answer,

' You know I was made for a pioneer, Carlo. I'll go to-morrow and send you word when I find work for us both. There are plenty of people passing this way from the southward.'

C. No, by Zeus, I won't stay without you. Let's

have one more day, and I'll go.   [After a pause.]   I say, dragoman, what's the English for *Ardilla*?

W. B. Squirrel.   Suppose we say a grey tree squirrel, as you want one for a lady.

C. How terribly sharp you're getting ground!

W. B. Then we start on Friday morning.   Is it a bargain?

C. If you hold to it.

Then the young man got into bed, thinking to himself, 'Confound the old Mentor!   He's right though.   I can't stand the fire of La Niña's eyes. Blue fire, by all that's celestial!   And what a golden glory of hair it is!   And what a fool I am!   I——'

But sleep overtook him at this juncture, and held the dominion till day began to dawn; when Carlo shouldered his rifle, stole down the wooden stairs, and made for the Eastern hills.

He strode across the plain, wishing to reach the hills before the sun was up.   A rush of horses through the damp grass gained upon him, and soon Alberto reined up at his side with a led horse.

Don A. On the table are *tortillas* and chocolate, friend; let us return.

C. A thousand thanks, Señor Don Alberto.   But I am weary of the plains.   I seek the mountains.

Don A. A lioness is in the spurs of Las Salinas.   We lost a full-grown steer not many days since.

C. Will you join me?   We might encounter your enemy.

But the horseman declined this invitation, and returned to his chocolate.

Invigorated with the clear morning air, and amused at the idea of Don Alberto stalking a puma, in his equestrian costume of short *chaquéta*, and *calzonéras*, adorned with silver buttons, and open at the outside seam, displaying the white linen drawers, the manifold deer-skin gaiter, and the light deer-skin boot with its huge jingling spur ; amused at this mental picture, the cynic pursued his way, worked up the course of a stream, and looking up, saw above him a proud stag, standing in a broad beam of the morning sun.   For an instant it returned his gaze, and then, with a toss of the antlered head, turned away, and was lost to sight.   He reached the eminence and looked round.   Undulating hills, bristling with crops of wild mustard, lay between him and the mountains. A few scrub oak were growing by the watercourses, round the bases of the hills.

Now the stag glided from a dark coppice on the eastern slope, bounded over a dry chasm, and up the flank of the opposite hill, in a series of great jumps ; so the sportsman knew that it was a black-tailed buck [*Cervus macrotis*].

On and on, bounding above the mustard crests, and followed by a switching sound, as the shrill stiff weed whistled in its track.

Carlo beat round the northern skirt of the hill, but before reaching the trail on the other side, he saw the stag across the next ravine, making his way over the hill beyond, and still due east.

So he stalked the deer till noon, when it no longer showed its heels aloft in air, but toiled wearily, dragging its branching horns through the relentless weed.

Now he knew that the buck would seek covert. Beyond them was a knoll with a crest of holm-oak, interspersed with grey boulders and clumps of juniper. The stag would rest in this pleasant spot. So Carlo crawled up the lee-side on hands and knees, and lurked behind a tree.

The sun is now due south. Foreshortened shadows fall dark and hard upon the ground. Certain that the game is close, Carlo stands there faint and weary, knowing that *la leona*, if she came that way, would try his nerve.

But the harsh short bark of the *coyote** comes down the valley, nearer and nearer: two, three, four, or five, running down a trail. On a sudden they come to a check. A harsh clamour ensues. They have chanced on a cross trail. ' So, so!' thinks the hungry man under the holm-oak, and cocks his piece.

Then the stag springs up from a covert close at hand, and stands with heaving sides, staring wildly up the pass. But a foe more terrible than the *coyote* is on his flank. The rifle's sharp crack rings a death-note in his ear. Down he lies: no bounding now: a quivering of limbs: a lolling out of the tongue: a glazing over of that splendid eye.

* *Lysiscus Caygottis.* Anglo-American, Prairie-wolf.

Carlo cooked and ate his kidney in the ravine, for there was water there.   Ever and again from the knoll above came the weird barking, a wild refrain; but a few strips of flannel swaying in the breeze secured his prize, and he again struck eastward.

Beyond the line of mustard, he found fair upland pastures, still farther a forest of white oak.   Here the tree squirrel sleeps away the afternoon in leafy solitudes.   At the least disturbance it awakes and utters a low soft whistle.

Such a sound now greeted his longing ears under the oak trees.   Then a pale grey shadow glided in and out among the branches.   He watched patiently where it disappeared.   At length the tip of a tail, rising a little, then a twinkling eye, peering under it.   Half an inch below; steady; fire!

So this wily sportsman knocked a bit of bark off under a squirrel's nose, and secured the timid animal without injury.   The tail was perfect: a brush of silver grey longer than the whole body.   Creeping down the back, too, new fur gave promise of a goodly summer coat.

Carlo hooded the grey friar with his tobacco-pouch.   'You little beggar,' he said, 'don't I envy you!' and turned homewards with a light heart.   But the light heart grew heavy as he went.   The cloud was over him again.   'Home,' he thought, 'what home?' and smiled bitterly.

But Don Guillermo breakfasted at the Rancho, and afterwards falling to work on the trunk of a tree

which was lying in the court, took what he was
wont to call 'a breather.' The three girls stood in
the upper balcony, overlooking his work. Julia on
one side, and Francesca on the other, each had an
arm round Nita's little waist. 'I won't stay,' she
said; 'I tell you I don't like him. He is cold, like
Estéban, and reads one's thoughts, like papa.'

'But you shall stay, *Niña de mis ojos!*' said Julia
softly. ' He is brave and gentle : and see how strong
he is!'

And still they looked on: but William, unconscious
of their looking, hewed and hacked away.

At the sound of horses approaching, the *donzellas*
fled : but Don Mariano, with a led horse, surprised
the Englishman at his work.

William mounted, and rode with his host down to
the sea-shore, and along the sand at a pleasant canter.
The swell broke on the shore with solemn thunder,
and sent its foaming flakes scudding at the horses'
feet. Don Mariano was riding the roan, William
a powerful chesnut. 'Civil fellow this Arianas,'
thought the latter; 'no humbug about him. Fine
beast this : splendid stride!'

'At how much do you value this horse?' he
asked.

'At the price of your acceptance,' was the ready
answer, as if the other had been reading his thought:
Alberto shall select a young horse for Don Carlos.
He is a light weight.'

'But we are *povres*,' pleaded William.

'You are rich in a service which I shall ask at your hands,' said the hidalgo.

And William said, 'It is granted before you ask.'

What the favour was which the rich man had to ask of the poor will be seen by-and-by. William in the meantime beguiled the dinner-hour by telling the story of their mining disaster.

'*Cuan presto se va el placer!*' said the Don, punning on his misfortune. But William garnished his tale with the exploits of Don Carlos—how he had fought a drawn battle with a bear, how he had prevailed against a warrior of the Crowfeet tribe, and made a friend of his vanquished foe. And you might have thought that the narrator had been sitting by all those months, with folded arms, or had · been looking on serenely from the heights of Mount Shasté or Olympus.

Alberto and Estéban were going to saddle some of the three-year-olds that afternoon : would Don Guillermo join them ? So the three young men rode off, with Cristóbal, the chief *vaquéro*; but the Señor would smoke his *cigarito* with the ladies.

As they rode away Don Mariano said to his wife, 'It is well. He goes to Santa Perona.'

'And Don Carlos ? '

'Goes with his friend.'

Whereupon Julia rose up and kissed Juanita's forehead; and the latter young lady clasped Julia's hand, pressed it to her lips and then to her breast, as much as to say, 'It is with love to you that my heart beats so.'

The family of Arianas were assembled for the evening meal when Carlo appeared in front of the *ramada.* The ladies greeted him : ' *Buenas tardes,* Don Carlos.' But Alberto said, satirically, ' *Buenas noches, señor.* '

' Come, señor,' said Madre : ' sit 'near to me, and relate your adventures. The lion has not killed you: but what ravens fed you in the desert ? '

' This hungry bird, señora,' he said, pointing to his rifle.

Don Mariano lifted the heavy piece curiously. ' And what food did it bring ? ' he asked.

' A kidney.'

' Kidney ? '

' From a black-tailed buck. But it was too heavy for the poor *Inglés*, or he would have laid it here.' And Carlo laid his battered *sombréro* at Madre's feet.

She smiled, and the Don thought within himself, ' *Bueno !* It is *caballéro*, this poor *Inglés*.'

' But if your Grace will lend me a little mule, I will return with the buck before the moon is over-head.'

William had come in meanwhile. ' We'll go together, Carlo,' he said ; ' I want to talk to you.'

Horses were at their disposal, and a sumpter mule. Don Mariano would accompany them, or Alberto. No, the Englishmen would not trespass on their kindness. A moonlit walk in the hills would please them well. *Una mulita*, as Carlo had said, to carry the buck : no more.

Then the hunter modestly unrolled a little bundle, and produced the hooded squirrel.

Every one looked except Juanita, who cast down her eyes ; and again her heart beat loudly.

'*Alma mia*,' said her mother. 'The *caballéro* is better than his word. See what he has brought you: *Ardilla bonita !* '

'A favour to your father's guest, señora,' he said, giving it into the young lady's hands.

Then she looked at him with a tear in her eye; and a little sigh, but no word escaped her lips. That sly fellow, Don Guillermo, had elevated his friend to the rank of a hero, you see.

Carlo has since been heard to say that at that moment he felt like a suddenly enriched pauper ; bewildered by a host of vivid sensations, 'wheeling with precipitate paces' through the brain. One brooding fear is present—the fear of waking to find it was a dream.

As far as one could observe, however, he was wide awake, and eating heartily, a moment afterwards ; saying little, for his stock of Spanish was small, and he was well aware that those supercilious Dons, Estéban and Alberto, would be glad to catch him tripping.

But now the sumpter mule is saddled. Don Guillermo declines the services of Cristóbal, the chief *vaquéro*. They will take no dogs. Only the large English pistols, which bite when they bark, and a little tobacco in Carlo's seal-skin pouch. Nita gives

it up reluctantly. She likes not this night wandering. Don Carlos is already tired. She wants no
venison. So she would tell Don Guillermo, if it were
not for that basilisk eye of Alberto watching her.

The two friends were accustomed to travel by
moonlight, with a sumpter mule. As they went, they
talked.

W. B. You saw the chesnut horse, with a star ?

C. Yes.

W. B. Up to my weight, think you? Suit me, eh?

C. Poor old boy ! I wish you may get it.

W. B. En effet, it's mine.

C. Yours ?

W. B. Yes ; and you're to have a *pinto*.

C. What's that ?

W. B. A piebald, with a wall-eye and a rat-tail.

C. And other amiable qualities ?

W. B. Yes : jumps bow-backed and stiff-legged,
lays back its ears, and squints horribly.

C. What a lark !

W. B. Zebra, you mean. Alberto held on by pum-
mel and cantle. Then I tried him.

C. Bravo, Briggs !

W. B. But I couldn't get him far. He stood up
on his hind legs, and struck out like a prize-fighter.
Then I pulled him over on the top of me ; and what
with that, and laughing at the brute, my sides have
ached ever since.

C. But you don't mean to say they've given us the
nags ?

W. B. It's a sort of retaining fee. There is method in the hidalgo's generosity. It seems that Alberto is about to come into his kingdom, which is an estate between Las Salinas and the next ridge, the ' Monte Diablo,' I think they call it. They have built a large *corral* and a little house there ; but it has never been stocked yet ; and we are going over to help Alberto. He has five hundred head of his own, and Mariano sends fifteen hundred to graze, for this place is over-stocked in the dry season.

C. Long live Alberto ! You'll be minister of the interior, I suppose, and I shall be intrusted with the portfolio of foreign affairs.

W. B. We shall have a rare time of it. There are pumas and grizzlies, wolves and jackals, Tulare Indians and Texan horse-thieves, to be repelled or exterminated.

Then William Briggs told his friend a sad tale which Don Mariano had confided to him during their morning ride. A notorious horse-thief, called 'El Yanqué' by the Spaniards, but ' Yankee Jim' in the North, had been pursued in the previous year by a party of Ranchéros, amongst whom was Don Mariano's only son. An encounter took place between El Yanqué with his desperadoes and the ill-armed but chivalrous Spaniards, in which the young Arianas was mortally wounded.

Then they mused for a time, each following the bent of his own thought, until William spoke again.

W. B. Alberto is a curious fellow, Carlo. When

Mariano told him to select a good horse for you, he said you should have '*El pinto, un caballo divinsimo.*'

C. I was rather rude to him this morning. He has been taking more interest in me than I care about, for the last few days. But that's all over now. When do we go?

W. B. Not till Wednesday. And look here, Carlo. I am going to take up the cudgels for Alberto. Say that Los Ojitos were the Governor's house, and little Nita my sister. Say she entertains a foolish preference for you, whose prospects are shady; you wouldn't press your chance?

C. Why do you ask me, Will? *Verbum sap.* I'll be downright rude to her; and there's an end of it.

W. B. You can ride the divinest *pinto*, and break him in: and there are the other ladies, you know.

Three or four hours passed; the mule with its load, and the men with theirs, drew near the pleasant house sleeping in calm moonlight; not a sound reached them, nor a human eye saw them; but William, reverting to the sore subject, said, 'Carlo, don't let anything come between you and me:' and the other answered, 'All right, old boy, trust me, and I'll be true.'

CHAPTER IV.

A CROSS.

And, like a lowly lover, down she kneels.

DON CARLOS adopted a different system of horse-breaking to that which was in vogue at Los Ojitos, and generally in Mexico and Spanish California.

The custom there is to lasso a young horse, and gradually to approach it, hand over hand along the lasso. If it permits you so to draw near, you slip on a halter, blindfold the horse, and saddle, while two men stand at the head coaxing and soothing it. Then you mount; the eye-cloth is removed; the horse stares wildly about, and starts off at full speed. You apply the end of a lasso, and goad with a spur, to maintain the idea that not the horse, but you, are making the pace.

But if a lassoed horse rejects your advances, another noose is cast round its legs; it is tripped up; the near-fore and off-hind legs are bound together, while another man halters and blindfolds it.

Bound in this way, it is allowed to rise, and the saddle is put on.

This latter was the process to which *el pinto* had been submitted with such unsatisfactory results.

But Carlo rode it for a day or two without the saddle, taught it to know his voice and to follow him on foot, or to come when he clapped his hands. Then he saddled, without blindfolding it or girding tightly. After that he tightened the girths a little, and put a sack of beans on the saddle. Lastly, he sprung into the saddle himself; but by that time the horse was accustomed both to man and saddle.

At Los Ojitos the gentlemen were wont to look in at the *ramada*, and to take a basin of milk porridge, *pinóle con léche*, at ten o'clock in the forenoon. One morning they were discussing this repast, and the ladies were amongst them, though not partaking of it, when a peculiar shout was heard; and the *pinto* came flying over the court wall with Don Carlos on its back.

The hand of the Señor was transferring a spoonful of porridge to his mouth; it was arrested midway, and the mouth slowly ejaculated, 'Ca-a-Rramba!' The wall was four feet high, and the idea of surmounting it without a ladder had not previously occurred to the Señor.

Leaving his horse at the sheds, Don Carlos came to the bower for a light. No, he will not take *pinóle*; he ate a *tortilla* for breakfast. He clapped his hands and the piebald trotted up and rubbed its head against his breast, awaiting his pleasure.

Again Don Mariano gave vent to his wonder; but

Julia came forward and gave the horse a piece of maize cake, and stroked it kindly, saying, '*Caballo buéno! Pinto bonito!*'

The ladies all knew the story of Alberto and William finding their match in this quiet horse. The Señor, having heard it from Cristóbal, told his wife, who told it to the girls; and they laughed together till the tears came into their eyes. They were pleased at the triumph of their surly guest, and would make allusions to Alberto's discomfiture. And their brother, being strong in 'badinage,' would give as good as he took.

But the younger lady shrank from these encounters. She dreaded the basilisk eye of Alberto. She had a secret, and felt sure that he knew it. And oh, if he were to banter her on such a subject, how could she bear it? She also knew that her father was a discerner of secrets; but that was another thing. Now, by some revulsion in her habit of feeling, she could have fallen at her father's feet and confessed the truth to him, while she would fain have concealed it from her mother. She felt, without stopping to think why, that her father, the shrewd man, trusted this stranger; and forgot that a man may be trusted by all, but only loved by one.

Those were restless days for Carlo, ill-conditioned fellow that he was. Every day his manner grew more cold and distant. He was still a puzzle to Mariano, who thought he could read a man as you would tell the points of a horse. The women set little theories on foot. Could one of them have said aught to pain him? Had Alberto or Estéban done so? Had he and his friend quarrelled? They were seldom together at that time. Had the *povre* formed an attachment in his land; and did one of them remind him painfully of the cruel one? That must be it. He avoided their society, only spoke to them when addressed, and then in a hasty and abrupt manner. He was a victim of Cupid, doubtless; pierced with a barbed arrow; and all attempts to draw it out increased his anguish.

But this legend only obtained in conclave. No one of them believed in it. 'He was so different the first few days,' Nita thought. Poor little parasite! In those few days she had spread a thousand twining tendrils; and what was there for them to enfold? She gave in her adhesion to the story of unrequited love, but had no faith in it.

In her heart rang the echo which his voice had wakened; a response deep and tender. A careless hand might have swept over the chords for ages; but would they have responded in such tones? What answer? There was no answer to her questionings, no evidence for hope to cling to; but hope was a living power; it could live, and would work, if she had strength to trust it; so she flung the whole energy of her mind and heart into this simple lesson, 'Hope,' or perhaps I should say 'Trust!'

And, poor weak child, as we may think her, and foolish, as in our self-sufficiency we may deem her wisdom, she had the strength of purpose to decide on one thing, and the strength of nature, or of grace, to do it.   And this was no light thing; it was giving herself, for good or ill, to one absorbing sentiment. And if the decision of her mother and those two whom she called her sisters must be taken, they would say it was for the latter, would weary her to give it up, perhaps, and might—a thing she could not bear—disparage him in their sadness.

So she kept it down, and overlaid it with sunny smiles and seeming merriment; thinking how easy it would be to take these off again, and be at her own sad silent level when alone.

And Carlo saw the painted coverlid, and took it for the colour of her heart, and as he tightened the girths and mounted the ' divinest *pinto*,' he thought to himself bitterly, ' It's all serene.   Dear old Bill is too punctilious.   It makes him fanciful.'   But if Carlo had known how the young lady squeezed the captive squirrel in her bedroom, and what large hot tears fell upon it, he might have owned that his friend was right, and that he was right for keeping faith with him, and avoiding her.

' The ladies want to give you a reading lesson,' William said to him one evening; but he shrank from them, and going out to where the brawling of the stream relieved his humour, spouted his ballads to the trembling stars.   Sad work he made of them, no doubt, pronouncing his Spanish in an uncouth way, and feeling more the power of the rhythm than the sense;

> The sad mechanic exercise,
> Like dull narcotics, numbing pain.

Meanwhile preparations were made for a start. Two thousand head of cattle were selected, herded together by day, and corraled together at night. As far as could be, the herd was made gregarious.

William became expert in driving cattle, but his friend was too impetuous. While the great herd moved slowly along, Carlo would pick out some straggler, dash at him with a loud cry, and drive him to the front. As he executed this flank movement, a young bull or steer would lower its head and charge; so that a diversion was created, and the *pinto* incurred terrible risks.

A calm energy and patience are the qualities, which make a good drover. If you urge cattle, they become angry, and scatter as soon as the ground affords an opportunity.

They were to take twelve horses, besides those which they rode, to the new Rancho; also four mules with pack-saddles to carry the luggage. But the brood mares were to be left at Los Ojitos for a time.

The day came at last. Such a long weary day for Juanita! Every one was in a bustle. Madre and the two elder girls made a mountain of *tortillas* and little maize puddings; packed a hundred little par-

cels, and these by fives in larger parcels; stowing
them in unfathomable saddle-bags.

Don Guillermo received a present of the most aro-
matic properties. It was a jar containing ten bundles
of *cigaritos*, rolled by fair fingers. For William had
by this time established friendly relations with them
all. With Nita he used to talk playfully, and help
her to keep that painted coverlid over her heart.
He knew her secret in part; but did not William
remember his 'grande passion'? — a much more
serious affair—and had he not outlived it? Love in
youth is like a frost in blossom time; that year the
bud withers, the tree bears no fruit, but grows and
gathers strength for the years to come.

But to-day it all seemed frivolous and utterly
wearisome to that weary little heart. She scarcely
heard what people said to her, there was such a ringing in her ears. And though she smiled, it was a
bitter smile, for she felt it was a lie. 'Why should
I belie my true, true heart?' she mused. 'Can I
not live and suffer; ay, and die? What is life?
Ah me! Ah me! But he, too, is sad. If he should
know I love, would it not cheer his heart? Courage,
courage! What return do I ask? A look, a word.
It is not much; yet how much! how much to me!'

In this way, or in some such way, the poor child,
in her bewilderment, tried to think. The power of
reason had deserted her. She was carried along by
a resistless impulse.

The moon was full. They intended to travel

through the night, and to camp at sunrise on the Estrella. There the cattle would rest or graze; the pasture was good, and the river would restrain their wandering; there they could lasso fresh horses, take breakfast and a *siesta*.

The *partida* was on the move. The *caballéros* had taken leave of the ladies and were getting to horse: Carlo's conscience smote him for want of courtesy. He had lingered, and was stammering out some thanks to Madre for all her kindness. Then he walked out moodily to the sheds, and found there a white figure standing by the horse.

Carlo would have avoided this interview. He knew who it was, and could not trust himself with her alone. Unlike hers was the love he felt for her. Stifled now by his promise to William, by his sense of honour, it smouldered like a hidden fire; and all around him wreathed the smoke of angry passion and impious complaint of wrong.

'Don Carlos,' she said.

C. Señora?

N. You will not think ill of me?

C. Of you?

N. I want you to accept something.

[Carlo was surprised, and in doubt.]

N. Why do you not speak? My heart is breaking.

C. I dare not speak. I must not say what I would.

Then lifting up both her hands, she drew nearer. He felt her breath on his mouth. 'Stoop, Don Car-

D

los,' she said, and put a cord round his neck. At the end of it was an amber crucifix which he had seen on her breast.

Then they stood silently gazing at one another. He held out his hand, and said '*Adios.*'

She took his hand in both of hers, fell down on her knees and kissed it. '*A-dios!*' she sobbed piteously; and a large warm tear fell on his wrist.

So he rode away, no longer moodily, and angry with his lot; but full of tenderness and hope.

Carlo rode by the side of his friend in the wake of the great herd, which surged to and fro like troubled waters in the pale moonlight; but his memory lingered under the dark shed; he could still see the white figure kneeling there with streaming locks, and hear her sobbing piteously. How should he tell William what had passed, how ask counsel of his friend? He could not tell him. He felt that it was to him alone this bounteous child had given all she had to give; that he could not share even the knowledge of it with another. '*Adios! Adios!* God guard thee, little one!'

The night was long and toilsome, but none worked more patiently, or felt less weary, than Carlo. Don Mariano wondered at him. William wondered at him. As the night wore on, Carlo began to hum old tunes, and talk to his friend of early days, and recall old memories of their boyhood.

And William thought, 'I can't make him out, tonight. Has anything passed between them? No; I have his word against that. He must forget her. It's well that we've got away.'

And Carlo would sometimes question himself: 'Have I broken faith with Will? Haven't I avoided her? Did I say anything then? No, I am blameless. It is a free gift. God guard thee, sweet giver!'

'I can't get the subject out of my head,' thought William, 'the poor fellow looks so happy. I wonder whether old Brownlow left him anything, after all. One has heard of such things before.'

Carlo had been adopted by Mr. Brownlow, an old friend of his mother's, but had given grave offence to his guardian, two years before our narrative opens. News of the old man's death reached them, a month ago, in San Francisco. Carlo was crushed with grief: 'You know it isn't the money,' he said to his friend; 'you never thought me mercenary, did you?'

CHAPTER V.

CUPID *VERSUS* PAN.

LET us pass over an interval of a few days, during which Don Mariano and Estéban have returned to Los Ojitos; Don Alberto has also ridden away and left our friends in charge.

We are now inland, between the two main ridges of the Coast Range; far from the hearing of the wave: nearer to the haunts of the grizzly bear and puma.

But it is broad daylight. The mighty hunters are in their fastnesses; and if it were not for a crowd of vultures, wrangling about the bones of a defunct steer, you would hear nothing but the lowing of kine in distant pastures, and a whisper of the little river Lorenzo in its grassy bank.

The house stands on a gently rising ground above the stream. It is a small cottage with high pitched roof, and a corridor in front, formed by the deep projecting eave. The roof is of red tiles, the walls of brown *adobés*, or unbaked bricks. The house faces and looks down the valley. At its back, or south side, is a clump of white oaks, among which a few tame cows are chewing the cud.

The interior of the house is in two compartments, of which the smaller is a bedroom. At about two feet from the ground, coarse pieces of sail-cloth, by way of beds, are stretched on rude frames of oak, and above one of them is a square window, with a wooden shutter. In the middle of this room stands a block with a basin on the top, and on either side of the door hang the implements of the toilet and the second flannel shirt. This is the sanctum of the two Englishmen.

In the middle of the larger room is a rude table, and round the walls are pegs and hooks of various sizes, for hanging up saddles and bridles, lassos, cooking utensils, tools, and what not.

The fire, burning night and day, is ten paces in front of the house. There is the cuisine, there the common rendezvous for food and gossip; around it men and dogs repose at night, and over it those nimble vestals, the *vaquéros*, keep continual watch.

We have left the fair sex on the shore of the much-resounding sea. Here we see nothing more like a vestal virgin than Cristóbal, standing in the camp-fire's ruddy glare, an hour after midnight, or folding his red *sarapé* round him in the morning mist.

William and his friend rise before the sun, walk a few paces down the stream to where the water is deep, plunge in and swim to the next rapids, then return with dishevelled locks and whetted appetites. The *pinóle con léche* is being gently stirred over the fire. They despatch a bowl of this delicious porridge,

and a broiled steak ; or if fresh meat is not to be had,
a twist of *carne secco,* and a gourd of milk.

Then the five horsemen scour the country, collect
the cattle in a hollow, and count them.   Cristóbal,
with one *vaquéro,* goes in search of the stragglers.
The Englishmen return with the other *vaquéro.*
Leaving him to yoke the draught oxen and follow,
they take their axes to a grove of beech and alder,
up the stream ; and soon the wood is ringing with
swift blows.   The saplings fall and are stripped of
their branches more quickly than Manuel can haul
them away ; but oxen are slow brutes when yoked ;
and dragging trees over rough ground is tiresome
work.

By-and-by our friends return to dinner, and be-
guile the moments with literature, or needlework,
while the *vaquéros* perform culinary parts.   But alas
for the bright-eyed naiads of the 'Little Springs,'
'the delight of subtle laughter, the delight of low
replies !'   They get through their ' pig-tail,' as Carlo
calls the *carne secco,* with a garlic or a few beans ;
and then to work again.   'One can't be always bill-
ing and cooing like those doves, you know.'

'At least, one isn't,' was the laconic answer ; and
again they scoured the country, collected and counted,
penned stragglers into the *corral,* and returned to the
great work.

It grows day by day.   A double row of beech stems
are planted firmly in the ground.   These are united
by cross-beams, forming ten stalls, each ten feet in

width. Sloping cross-beams above form the roof, thatched for the time being with miscellaneous branches. The back and sides are filled in with tall willow stakes, which will soon take root, and spread tough shoots, so as to form a living wall.

Here they work till the sun is low on the ridges of Las Salinas: then leaving Manuel to prepare for supper, they gallop away to collect and count once more. There are stragglers to be found, driven in, and corraled, the whole herd to be counted, the *caballáda* to be driven in, and fresh horses lassoed for the next day's work.

Man and horse is weary: night is wearing away; Manuel sleeps over his mess of meat and beans; round the herd a thousand *coyotes* hover with weird lamentations, wailing for their prey.

At length supper is despatched. The long valley glimmers in the misty moonlight: at its head stand the little house and long range of sheds; a camp-fire flaring in their angle, and the dim forms of prostrate men and dogs. The cattle are slumbering in the dewy grass, a mile below; but five tame cows, with their calves, are among the clump of oaks near the house.

The dogs whine in their sleep: their muzzles are distorted with fear. The figure of Cristóbal rises from the earth, steals noiselessly to the house and enters.

' *La lova !*'

On a sudden, a sharp crash and a fearful howl ring

through the stillness; the howl is taken up for miles around, and in amongst the mountains by innumerable voices. Such a wail! You might have thought the last trump had sounded, and that the sons of perdition answered to their doom.

As it died away, Carlo drew his rifle in at the window, and said to William, 'Look at that fellow, Cristóbal.'

So William looked out and saw the grim *vaquéro* skinning a huge grey wolf, by the light of the moon. 'The hide is no use, you know, if it's left on,' he said; and they coiled themselves up again to sleep.

But Don Alberto, as we have said, had ridden away. The *caballéro* did not return to Los Ojitos with his brothers, but turned his horse's head to the south-west, in the direction of San Luiz Obispo. It was the time of the Carnival. There was much dancing, guitar-strumming, and serenading going on at the time. For instance, one evening a ball took place at the house of Don Bernardo, the merchant. The élite of San Luiz were there. The daughters of the merchant were adored of all. '*Graciosas son estas muchachas*,' was agreed on all hands; and in a future chapter we shall hear the Doña Barbara introduced as 'La Graciosa,' as though she were the type of certain faculties which that word expresses. But Alberto was attached to the Doña Isabel.

Was that Philomel, warbling in the garden, near the lattice of the Señorita, when the moon was low?

A sonorous tone rolled above the silent shadows; and in its wake rang tremulous chords, as of a stringed instrument. If you had shared the bower of the melodious wooer, you might have seen, at an open window, a white figure standing in pensive mood, half shrouded by deep clusters of drooping hair; then you might have seen a small hand pressed to lips, and waved towards the bower, and nothing more; still that was much to Philomel.·

At another time the Doña Isabel sat on a gorgeous ottoman, striped with crimson and yellow damask. At her foot, on a cool Chinese mat, a gentleman reclined on his stomach and elbows, with his face raised to her knees, and his eyes to her face, which drooped towards him.

'Unkind!' he said. [The lady looked anything but that.]

'Señor?'

'Call me Alberto, or I die.'

'I am not cruel, Don Alberto: I may not disobey.'

'Alas! I thought that love was free.'

'Is Alberto free?'

'Bound to thee, *vida mia!*'

'And loving the bond?'

How could the bondsman endure such a question? He laid his forehead down upon her knee, and groaned. So she passed her soft fingers through his hair, lifted up his head, and looking down into his dark eyes asked—

'Wouldst thou suffer loss to keep the bond?'

'Rancho, cattle, horses, all ! '

'*Ahora, créo que me quieres.*' ('Now I believe that thou lovest me.')

She kissed his low brown forehead and patted his head; but the lover, stooping down in ecstasy, kissed her feet. Whereupon the lady screamed; and Barbara, running in, saw this amusing tableau, which makes her laugh even to the present day, she is so vivacious.

Towards the end of February, Alberto returned to Santa Perona. He was in high spirits, but took little interest in his Rancho. He looked languidly on the new sheds, languidly on the cattle. He saw and, for a day or two, shared the labour of his friends. '*Es muchisimo travajo,*' he remarked, and thought to himself, '*Caramba!* I love not work,' but did not say so; it was sufficiently evident.

Then William pressed him on the wants of the estate. A waggon was indispensable. The mules might be broken to harness, or a yoke of oxen would draw it. Their ammunition was failing. They also wanted strychnine to poison the wolves and *coyotes.* In spite of their vigilance, five yearlings had already fallen. It would be worse when the dry season came, and the bears would fall upon the cattle, which would then stray in search of pasture.

'*Es nada*—It is nothing,' replied the Ranchéro. 'What matter a few poor beasts ? '

W. B. The axes and knives are almost useless: we have rounded their edges with the soap-stone. You must have a grindstone on the Rancho.

Don A. But there are sandstones at the mission of San Miguel, *amigo*: send a *vaquéro* with a mule, and beg one of the Fray Don Antonio.

W. B. We want nails too. We must build a boundary house: ['*Caramba!*' interrupted the other.] We shall want a two-handled saw. And why should provisions be bought at the Pueblo? It is not too late. Is there not yet a fall of rain in April? Let us have a harrow, and seed, barley, maize, buckwheat.

Don A. But the unblest cattle will destroy the crops. Walls of *adobés* will hardly suffice to keep them out.

W. B. Above the valley is a glade difficult of access. One man might guard it well. The soil is fine. A stream waters it. Nature favours the enterprise.

They rode up to the glade and examined it. It was as William said. The Englishmen should have their own way. Don Guillermo should give him a list of what they required. *Que carajo!* He would sell a hundred head of cows—two hundred! A drove, on its way to the mines, would pass their old camp on the Estrella to-morrow: he would join them with two hundred head, and would return before the end of March.

'Alberto's is quite a limited monarchy,' said Carlo, after he had gone.

W. B. He is his own minister of finance, at any rate.

C. Worse luck.

W. B. You won't think me inquisitive ?

C. No.

W. B. What was that commission you asked him to execute ?

C. A little parcel for Los Ojitos, to be left at San Miguel. I had to tell him a lie about it: but I've kept faith with you, old boy, and swallowed a bitter pill.

The truth is, Carlo had reflected on the possession of the amber cross, and sent it back. ' It's something I brought away by mistake,' he said to Alberto; at which the other curled his moustache incredulously, but promised to leave the parcel with the Fray Don Antonio, to be forwarded.

CHAPTER VI.

FORTUNE SMILES.

INSTEAD of standing at the full length of their tether, shivering in the early dews, the horses now lay comfortably in their stalls, and in the day-time found rest there and shelter from the sun. The calves of the tame cows were also stalled, partly for their security and in part to prevent the cows from roaming. A nucleus of living creatures was also formed. The *caballáda* and the mules would hover round, the draught oxen were more frequently at hand ; and when the great herd was in danger from bear or puma, it would move up the valley towards the stronghold.

Their next object was to have a *vaquéro* settled at the northern boundary of the estate. Some one would be required there to keep a check on the cattle, when the extreme vigilance of the first few weeks had been relaxed.

The valley, as far as a stream which formed its northern limit, was six miles in length and a league in average breadth. It would be well to construct dams and artificial pools along the course of the stream, to secure water as the season advanced; for on the west were wide slopes and undulating sand-hills interspersed with large lagoons; on the east were the timbered slopes and foot-hills of the Sierra del Monte Diablo: on either hand was danger.

So they set to work and built a log-house on a knoll near the boundary, having so chosen the position that a column of smoke ascending from it might be seen at head-quarters.

The wily Cristóbal never flagged in merriment, seeing his future home arise. At Los Ojitos he had a wife and little boy. Here, Cristóbal thought, they should live and be happy; he would gamble no more at the Pueblos, but would work, and save, and become a man of substance, and, who could tell? some day he might rise to the rank of a *mayordomo*.

While Manuel would broil the meat or boil the tea, Cristóbal taught the Englishmen to throw the lasso. As soon as they could throw with certainty on foot, he allowed them to practise from the saddle, which they found easier, having a better elevation, and being already good horsemen. *El castaño*, William's horse, had been trained before; *El pinto* would now stand like a rock when the cast was made; though he and his rider got many a roll together, and learnt their business at the risk of their bones.

They were anxious to instal Cristóbal in the log-house; but without power and lead, he would be helpless in case of a raid. They ought also to have sky-rockets. With their small force, so divided, and with no rapid communication, every horse and mule might be swept off the *Rancho* in a single night.

It was the middle of March. The chances of Alberto's return before the April rains were passing away, and, with them, the opportunity of securing a harvest this year.

The Englishmen discussed these things with Cristóbal, who entered eagerly into all their plans. William informed him that *los Americanos*, who were settling in the valley of San José, harvested fifty and sixty fold for every *fanéga* sown ; and stated his conviction that the mountain glade was finer soil, and would yield more. Manuel and Francisco had seen as much at San Miguel, when they were *muchachitos*, in the good days before the missions had been despoiled. Carlo wondered whether Don Bernardo would let them have seed on credit. He was reported to be an enterprising merchant, and to cultivate a garden at the Pueblo de los Angeles.

One hot evening, as the baffled Carlo, with slouched hat and tattered shirt, stood in the corridor, a silent horseman reined up before him in a cloud of dust, and having handed him two letters, sped on his way. Carlo turned them over with trembling fingers. One was for William, the other for him. He opened it, and read as follows :—

' *San Francisco, Feb.* 12, 1852.

'Dear Sir,—As the steamer which drops the mail-bag at Monterey will sail early to-morrow, I write in haste to inform you that I have received advices from England, to the effect that you are entitled to a sum of 500*l*., as legatee, under the will of the late Mr. William Brownlow. The sum is now at your disposal, and can be transferred to your order, on my receiving the enclosed receipt with your signature. There are certain conditions attached to the transfer, which I need scarcely allude to, as you have long since complied with, or I may say anticipated them. Your trustee, Lord Saltum, expresses a great interest in you. He wishes to hear of your welfare; and I think it would please him if you were to write and treat him with some confidence, as the friend of your late lamented guardian. William will tell you that I am pressing upon him the value of land in this country, and the favourable opportunities which there are for investments of that nature. Allow me to assure you that my sister will always be pleased to entertain you at Los Dolores, and that you may command the services of

           ' Yours faithfully,

               ' T. S. STARCHIE.

' C. B. Melnot, Esq., care of
      Señor Don Alberto Arianas,
        Santa Perona.'

' Bill,' shouted the legatee, ' Bill! Yoix!'

' That's me,' answered William, milking a cow in the stalls and regardless of grammar.

' Letters! Look sharp.'

' Hurrah!' cried the dairyman, dropping the pipe out of his mouth, and kicking over the milk-pail.

Carlo tossed him the other letter, and retired to his room to read again. It was some time before he could realise the contents of the letter. The late Mr. Brownlow and Viscount Saltum, together with any interest they might have taken in him, were phantoms of the past. He conjured up the memory of a youth, gay, idle, self-indulgent, and reckless; but failed to recognise himself. 'I'm a thorough workman,' he thought; 'I like my pipe, it's true, and I've a horrid temper; but my habits are simple, and I've resisted the sweetest temptation man ever had. And it isn't over yet. Those mountains are a molehill. I kick them aside. I'm near her again, in the low dark shed. I feel her breath, her touch, her tear, her sobs. O Jesu! a little grace, a little strength!' And the young man took a wooden cross from his bosom [it was a model of the one in amber], kissed it, knelt down with his head on the rude tressel, and sobbed and sobbed. His lithe wiry form quivered with emotion; his throat felt as though it would burst, and a froth settled on his lip.

'Good news, Carlo!' shouted William from the corridor.

'Wait—a—minute—old—boy,' said the other; and he got up from his knees, sponged his head and face with cold water, and went out, humbled, but stronger, to do or to endure.

And William said, 'Here's something that will interest you.' And Carlo read as follows :—

E

' San Francisco, Feb. 12, 1852.

' My dear William,—I enclose a letter for you which came yesterday under cover to me, and which will no doubt give you good news from home.   As I have not heard from your father by this mail, I shall be glad to hear of him from you, at your leisure.   I received your letter from Los Ojitos by the steamer which touched at Monterey.   You can communicate with me regularly by the same medium.   I was surprised to find that you had not availed yourselves of my letter of recommendation to Don José, and it is curious that you should have received such marked hospitality and kindness from the family of Arianas, as you must be perfect strangers to them, although they are connected with my good friend Don José. The connection is a delicate one ; and you had better be guarded in alluding to it, or perhaps you should abstain altogether from the subject with your present host.

' The Doña Juana (Madre) of whom you spoke in such flattering terms is the only sister of Don José. [" By Jove, he's *her* uncle, then ! " said Carlo parenthetically.]   Don Mariano met her at the house of General de Castro in Monterey.   An attachment sprung up between them, which was cemented by a private marriage [O-ho!], and clandestine interviews, which lasted during the month of February 1835, after which the lady returned to her father's house.

' When the old Señor Don Joaquin, who was the leader of the Federal, or Ecclesiastical, party in this country found that his daughter had contracted an alliance with the son of a notorious Republican and lay impropriator, his fury exceeded all bounds. He drove his child, with threats and abuse, out of his house [The old rogue!]; and as Don José was at that time in Spain, the poor lady was indebted to the kindness of an Indian *vaquéro*, employed on the boundary of the estate, who conveyed her in safety to the mission of San Miguel. [Bravo, Friday!] When Don Mariano found that his wife had been so harshly treated, he was naturally both mortified and grieved; but, with the courtesy of a true Castilian, he forbore to demand satisfaction of her father, and sent his challenge to Don José [Rum go, that!] on his return to the country. The result was an encounter of the most courtly kind. Don José, an accomplished swordsman, disarmed his opponent. Don Mariano's second declared that the affront was cancelled, and there the matter ended. The brothers-in-law, however, did not exchange further courtesies, nor can they do so until Don José further disarms his antagonist, by apologising for the affront which the Señor Don Joaquin put upon the lady. Don José has allowed me to understand that he has no objection to make this *amende* [Bravo, Don!], but that it would not be decorous to do so during his father's lifetime.

'You see that the code of honour amongst our friends is somewhat punctilious. Now you will have to exercise discretion in the delicate position in which you are placed, unless you like to forego the pleasure

of an acquaintance with Don José. Their estate,
the *Hacienda* of San Pedro, abuts on the *Rancho* of
Santa Perona. [Hallo! now the cat's out.] Don
Alberto and his *vaquéros*, as well of course as Mr.
Melnot and yourself, will frequently be brought in
contact, from the straying of cattle and so forth,
with Don José and his Indians. The gentlemen
cannot acknowledge each other under existing circumstances, and I fear that you might wound the
feelings of Don Alberto by establishing a friendly intercourse with his neighbour. Yet I feel, as your
friend, that, if possible, you should establish such an
intercourse [Sensible old party!]; so, now that you
know the difficulty, I must leave you to act *à dis-
crétion.*

'The offer of remuneration which Don Mariano
has made you is handsome, and speaks for his
generosity and confiding disposition; for, as I said
before, both Mr. Melnot and yourself must be total
strangers to him. [Fancy not trusting Bill!] And
now I will again press upon you the value of an in-
vestment in land. [Eh?] You will have ample
opportunities for observing the quality and suitable-
ness of the land for many miles round; and remember that any land not now occupied, or for which the
present holder cannot produce clear title-deeds, may
be purchased, and the sale carried out here in a few
weeks, at $1¼ per acre. [Hurrah!]

'When I was on a visit at San Pedro, last month,

I rode over to Santa Perona and saw the fine corral, and humble cottage which had been built upon it. The estate has great capabilities; and you might perhaps purchase a few thousand acres to the southward [Exactly: and a chain of mountains or two !], and profit by the kindness and experience of Don Alberto [O dear, yes !] in getting it into working order.

' I will not describe the estate of San Pedro, as I hope before long you may make its acquaintance for yourself. Nor will I protract this already tedious letter [No, no !] by encroaching on one which I am about to write to your friend, and which he will doubtless read to you. I am, dear William,

' Your very sincere friend,

' T. SYLVESTER STARCHIE.'

When William had finished the paternal letter, his friend said to him, ' Is old Starchie mad; or have you come into a park and ten thousand a year ?'

W. B. No, he 's all right. I have got a little money ; nothing to speak of.

C. How much is it ?

W. B. You mustn't press me just now. My way is not quite clear. You see, there are ten of us.

C. True : at any rate, we'll invest my 500*l.*

W. B. I think we might venture in a little joint-stock company transaction. Say, you divide your fund, and lay 250*l.* by for a year. I could add 250*l.*

to the other half, and we might buy a few cows or pigs.

C. If we look sharp, we may get that glade sown with barley or maize yet.

W. B. I'm afraid not.

C. [Referring to a shabby almanac.] Look here. Steamer up from San Luiz on the 16th. Get to San Francisco on the 18th. Draw money; consult Starchie; buy no end of things; take Panama steamer down on the 21st. Cristóbal meet you at San Luiz with mules. In meantime I harrow the ground. Lay the seed down directly you get back. April rains come just in the nick of time.

W. B. You are not far out, barring accidents.

C. Well; let's bar them. When will you start?

W. B. To-morrow, at daybreak.

After the duties of that day were ended, the two friends sat, late into the night, talking over their camp-fire.

W. B. Will you go instead of me?

C. No: I'd rather stay here. You go, and I'll scratch up that glade a bit.

W. B. There's Miss Clem, you know.

C. Shut up: that's a good fellow.

W. B. How many pigs did you say?

C. The more the merrier: but remember the Panama Line 'sticks it on' awfully.

W. B. Don Bernardo may know of a litter or two at San Luiz. That would save freightage.

C. Well: we've acorns enough for the whole

species.* [Lights his pipe during a pause.] I say, isn't that Don Bernardo a friend of Alberto's?

W. B. Yes. [Another pause. Both puffing away solemnly.]

C. By the way, what did Alberto say about 'Yankee Jim'?

W. B. The Committee of Vigilance have offered a reward for his body. There's a placard stuck up in all the Pueblos and missions about it. Alberto says he's not unlike me, according to the description of him.

C. That's the man who killed the poor Don's only son.

W. B. Yes.

C. I don't envy the fellow who lays a hand on him.

W. B. The *quinientos pésos* will do it. Eh, Cristóbal?

And looking at the *vaquéro*, they observed an ominous look about his bright eyes and bristling moustache. He too had heard Don Alberto speak of the five hundred dollars; and certain it is that the honest half-caste would have engaged his Satanic Majesty in single combat, for that sum of money.

But the Englishmen went on talking in their own language, and thought no more about Cristóbal.

C. I hope 'El Yankee' won't come this way while you're gone. A bear's a bear, you know, but —— but——

---

* The white oak of this region is the *Quercus longiglanda*; acorns sweet, from two to three inches in length.

And William, who knew what his friend was thinking about, changed the subject.

Before daybreak the house and sheds were swathed in a grey mist, which came up from the river. Francisco was going as far as the Puerto del Oso with Don Guillermo. · They were saddling the horses.

C. [Shivering.] I ·can afford to do one or two little things now.

W. B. That depends.

C. Yes; on your getting to San Francisco and getting the money. You know we're going to have Angela over.

W. B. Yes.

C. And Cristóbal got broke the last time he was in Monterey.

W. B. Yes.

C. So you can buy them a few things for me: blankets and cotton-prints and stockings.

W. B. And a soup-kitchen ?

C. No chaff now. And you remember the ladies saying they wanted books ?

W. B. Can't say I do.

C. Now don't be obstinate. Buy five pounds' worth, and a set of Chinese chessmen for the Don. You can leave them at Monterey as you come down the coast.

W. B. Five pounds would buy two pigs.

But Carlo disposed of the possible pigs by the aid of a strong monosyllable, and the two friends parted.

CHAPTER VII.

A MELODIOUS CHAPTER.

WILLIAM BRIGGS was one of those characters whom one only meets in books, and in odd corners of the world. What good fortune came to him he took with a good grace : ill fortune found him stout-hearted and imperturbable. He was very patient too, and would endure for a long time unconsciously. So he was slow in forming plans of action, having a floating notion in his brain that we do not form our own plans at all, but are impelled in one direction or another. ' Happy go lucky ' is the expression applied to his philosophy by cautious people.

Free from vanity, he cared little what impression he made upon other people, but was entirely loyal to himself. An American writer speaks of men who shout, to hear the echo of their own voices. William was not one of these. He could shout lustily, and did so when there was any occasion for it, but neither knew nor cared how his voice sounded, nor what tricks the ' reverberate hills ' might play with it. This carelessness of approbation sat well upon him. Nature is more dignified than Grandison, more graceful than Chesterfield.

Now he rode away in the dim morning and mused,

'Impetuous fellow Carlo is! I like it in him though. He's worth a dozen of that brother of his; the demure prig! And really just now it's well to have some one to look after. It is not well for an old patriarch like me to have no one but himself to think about.' Meanwhile the long shadows of William and his guide moved solemnly before them through the waste; the tinkling of their spurs* and bridle-reins sounded sadly in the solitude.

'The Governor's right. I may as well have young Tom out. That will be one provided for. And now the Governor has got a County Court, and Ned his scholarship, they won't want my money. Won't the young rascal enjoy this life, coming to it with a fresh heart and mind! I wish they had done something of the kind with me. Court scandal sears the heart, and poetry softens the brain. I was not cut out for a Secretary of Legation.'

And indeed William was not an astute personage; but had passed his noviciate in the Diplomatic Service chiefly in translating the odes of Quintus Horatius into appropriate Castilian verse, and the *Romancéros* of Andalusia and Castile into appropriate English. We do not say that no wind had ruffled the calm surface of such a life: but we cannot be continually storm-tost.

That afternoon Don Bernardo was entertaining

* The Mexican spur is silver, and has enormous rowels, with two little silver acorns dangling from the centre. From the bit the first eight inches of the bridle are a chain of steel or silver.

three cavaliers with a glass of choice Bordeaux. Enters to them a tall stranger, with grey eyes and tawny beard, who lifts a much-worn *sombréro*, wishes them *Buénos dies*; and can they tell him if Don Bernardo is within ?

The merchant rises and returns the salutation. Can he serve the señor ?

William wishes to know if there is a light waggon and harness for a pair of mules to be sold in San Luiz. He is going by steamer to San Francisco, to make some purchases; hopes to return on the 23rd instant, and would save the expense of bringing a waggon from the metropolis.

'Will the señor step across to the *Plaza* ? Here is a perfect set, left by the Quartermaster's baggage train, to be sold on commission. The harness with breast-straps : will that suit ? '

' Perfectly. And the price ? '

' Two hundred dollars, complete.'

The stranger winces, but preserves his composure, remembering that 'the Panama Line sticks it on awfully.' 'Will Don Bernardo keep it till the 23rd ? '

' Certainly. For the Señor Don —— ? '

' Guillermo.'

' Then I address the mayordomo and friend of Don Alberto ? '

' The same.'

' Your hand, Don Guillermo : I too am an Englishman.'

And as the two men, till now strangers to each

other, stood hand in hand, the waggon, the harness, the stunted sycamores, the broad Plaza, the very vault of heaven, faded out of sight. The 'death in life' lived again, 'the days that are no more.'

By-and-by, when the grave and reverend signiors had discussed matters of importance, William was introduced to the ladies, with whom he conversed (in Spanish), and to whom he sang, by request, a song in the English idiom, which I shall take leave to insert. It may help us to interpret William's humour.

> Why not reminded be of hours so brief
>   And glorious?
> Dwells not a beauty in the autumn-leaf;
> And, over memory's lingering joy, is grief
>   Victorious?
>
> Is there no meaning in the having been
>   Once blessed?
> Can winter leaves still hold a summer green;
> Or think you ancient wrongs have never been
>   Redressed?
>
> Doth not joy linger in the silver cones
>   Of mountains,
> Which gleam in sunlight of the western zones,
> While o'er the plain night sweeps with all its moans
>   Of fountains?

When the music ceased, the sad humour seemed to have fallen upon all, and presently the boom of a cannon surprised them in silent reverie.

Don B. Ah! There is the steamer. We must lose you so soon.

Señoritas. But you will come again ?

W. B. Yes.

Señoritas. And make us all cry again ?

W. B. Never. Forgive me this time.

So William went on board, with the mail-bag, and not being a victim to sea-sickness, smoked his cheroot in the bows.

The doubts about Alberto were cleared up. Don Bernardo was commissioned to sell the *Rancho* of Santa Perona, with two hundred cows, for twenty thousand dollars, a liberal discount allowed for ready money. 'And, as the Governor says, I ought to cast anchor somewhere or other. I shall be as old as the Wandering Jew soon : [Looking down,] by Holy Rood, a royal beard ! I must consult Mariano before buying this place. Won't he thunder out his *carambas!* Suppose it's all square between Bernardo and his client : Alberto smitten of course : Bernardo take him into partnership : money at a premium : sell cattle : sell *Rancho* : turn the money over in no time: suit that lazy *iguana.*

'I could graze Mariano's stock gratis, take Carlo into partnership ; and then we might think about the little one. Yet I wish it had been Julia. She has that repose which Carlo wants. His pulse beats very fast.'

Then William walked aft, and turned into his berth ; for he had ridden twenty leagues, in the heat of that day ; and now a cold nor'-wester was sweeping the surface of the sea.

The next evening, at sunset, they steamed into the Golden Gate, and William was welcomed by his father's friend. But Miss Clementina Starchie was shocked at the appearance of the gentleman, who once had inhaled the sublime atmosphere of Courts. 'O William!' she said, 'how can you go about in that old *thing* [a flannel shirt], and those dreadful Hessians?'

' "Jacks," we call them,' William objected.

'Indeed?' And the damsel fell to thinking of a magnificent hidalgo, with curling hair and purple moustachios, who had galloped away with papa on New-year's Day; who with his *sombréro* had described a splendid arc, and bent his head to the saddle-bow as she stood blushing in the porch.

What a vision it was! There was a murmur of canzonets and serenades about the very memory of it, and—only look at poor William!

But Aunt Dorothy was charmed to entertain the light-clad hero.

Clementina was at that time a beautiful little fairy of nineteen years. Her hair was yellow, her forehead broad and white, eyebrows yellow and arched, eyelashes black; eyes large, brown, and lustrous; nose celestial, lips ravishing; and there was such a dimple in the little round white chin, that a man might have wished to touch it and die.

Clemmy was sad to think she had received William coldly, and after tea she said to him, 'Come and talk to me about your new life. I must write

and tell Annie all about you.' And William talked
to her, and wondered at her self-conscious manner
and downcast eyes and flushing cheek.

W. B. And do you know, Clem, I sang one of my
translations from Don Jorge to three English *señoritas*
in San Luiz, and they all cried.

Cl. Your songs *were* very——

W. B. Yes.

Cl. At least we used to think so.

W. B. Don't say ' we.'

Cl. Well, *I* thought so, William.

W. B. That sounds more pretty. But the oddity
of their crying was, that they couldn't understand a
word of English.

Cl. English ladies—did you not say ?

W. B. You see, their mother was a Mexican, and
Don Bernardo, their papa, has left off his English
habits. However, mine was a voice out of the past.
They heard it and wept. Why, you're crying too !
Dear Clem, what have I said to hurt you ?

Cl. Nothing—nothing ; come and sing.

And she went and sat down at the piano, took off
a little bracelet which William had given her years
ago, held it for a moment irresolutely, then looked up
into his calm face.

' William,' she said.

W. B. Well, dear ?

Cl. You are sad.

W. B. Well ?

Cl. I know the cause.

W. B. Yes.

Cl. And I am not all a—a sister ought to be to you, all that Annie would be; but, dear William, will you give me one 'yes' or 'no,' truly?

W. B. Truly.

Cl. Is there anything I can do, or say, or *be*, to comfort you? Tell me truly.

W. B. Nothing, dear little sister, nothing.

And William took the little hand still holding the bracelet, stooped over it, and kissed it tenderly.

'Eh? Bless my soul!' exclaimed papa, awaking out of a nap.

'The custom of the country, sir,' said William, smiling.

But Clem ran across the room, clapping her hands, and laughing: 'O, papa! I'm so happy! I've offered to run away with William, and he won't.'

And William saw that she said it half in sport, half in earnest, and admired the little heroine.

There was a secret between these two. William, five years ago, had loved Clem's elder sister. The intimacy grew and deepened; but an estrangement took place, and the lady became another man's wife.

And now Annie Briggs had written to Clem, and had said, 'Be a sister to him, or more than a sister. As you are better and more beautiful than I, be to him more than I have ever been. I fear for the effect of a grief, which he will not share with anyone, on his health and mind, though nothing can taint or alter his true pure heart.'

So the little woman covered up the image of a magnificent hidalgo, with raven moustaches, in a dark corner of her heart, and made an advance to her friend's brother, with result as above.

Then she returned to the piano.

'Sing Mr. William the *Cancion* which he translated for you,' said Aunt Dorothy.

'O, the poor convict's lullaby? No, it is too sad. I set it to music myself, William.'

'I gave you the words. Give me the song.'

And the lady sang this lullaby :—

> Fair galley, rest
> In the golden west !
> Lull him to sleep,
> On the cold calm breast
> Of the passionless deep :
> Lull him, O lull him to sleep !
>
> Ah me ! ah me !
> Would that I, with thee,
> Might float at rest !
> For the lone sad sea
> Bears my love on its breast.
> Lull him, O lull him to rest !
>
> Spread thy broad sail
> To the morning gale !
> Come to thy rest !
> A breeze shall not fail
> Thee, all day from the west.
> Lull him, O lull him to rest !

F

Fair galley, glide,
On a tranquil tide,
  Home to thy rest!
The haven is wide,
And my sheltering breast
Yearns till it lull him to rest.

O sleep, love, sleep
Once more in the deep
  Of my still breast!
While I weep, love, sleep,
In my fond arms prest,
Lull'd in my bosom to rest!

But sentimental evenings, like æsthetic and all other evenings, must come to an end. And when Don Guillermo made his appearance before Clem, on the following afternoon, he was dressed as became a cavalier and *Ranchéro* of substance: that is to say, in a linen shirt, a short blue jacket, blue *calzónes* supported at the waist by a gorgeous sash, and dangling about the legs, with an exterior descent of silver buttons, waxing 'small by degrees and beautifully less.' The 'Hessians' also were replaced by deerskin ankle-boots.

In the interval he talked matters over with Mr. Starchie, made arrangements for purchasing the estate of Santa Perona, bought seeds of many kinds, ammunition, tools, and other things useful; not forgetting five pounds' worth of books, or the 'Chinese chess-men for the Don.'

Owing to the kindness of a common friend, I am

enabled to place before the reader a copy of a letter which Miss Clementina wrote to Miss Annie Briggs, at about this period.

> *Los Dolores, near San Francisco,*
> *20th March.*

'My lovely Annie will be surprised to hear that William is now spending a few days with us. We were quite startled when papa brought him home day before yesterday. And do you know—but how could you, so far away in dear Worcestershire?— that he wears a faded shirt the colour of blotting-paper, and great boots which come up ever so high, and no coat at all, and such a hat! And O, my dear Annie, when William landed he was nearly being taken for a horse-stealer: a dreadful creature called "Yankee Jim," who kills people and sells their horses; and papa says the Vigilance Committee would have hanged William if he had only had an anchor tatooed on his left arm. Can you imagine anything so wicked? Not that I believe a word of it. But now William has bought some beautiful clothes, and looks like one of those cavaliers who used to fight for King Charles against the vulgar Roundheads. And his voice is so touching; it reminds me of my sweet Annie and the dear old Christmas holidays! I did not tell you in my last what a beautiful grand piano papa has had brought from New York, all round Cape Horn, in a ship. It is handsomer and better toned than our old Collard, and I played William's accompaniments on it last night to the dear old songs which my Annie was so fond of.

'But what *do* you think? That friend of William's ("Carlo," as he calls him), that dreadful young man who was so wicked in India, and whom you wanted William never to speak to again, has had some money (papa won't tell me how much) left him by old Mr. Brownlow, who paid his debts and "cut him off with a shilling," you know, dear; and he and William are going to buy a *Rancho*, that is, a great wilderness with a few cows and horses straggling about it, and all sorts of wild beasts carrying them off; and papa says they will make a large fortune in a few years.

'We are all going to spend the months of June and July on an estate called San Pedro, with friends of papa's. It is only a few miles from the *Rancho* which William is going to buy. There we shall see the Indian corn gathered by real Indian squaws, and pumpkins in which a baby can lie down and be covered up, and great water-melons, and a tame puma, or "lion," as it is called; and we shall be able to ride to William's house—at least he says it's only "a hut," and—O, no, we mustn't, because of that Carlo, you know, dearest.

'I shall write and tell you more about William then, and about Mr. Melnot—what sort of person he really is. We have never seen him, though they were four days in San Francisco, after they lost all their gold—poor things!—in the mines. Papa asked William to bring him to dinner; but he would not come, and stayed sulking (though I pitied him then, because he had no money) at a common tavern in the horrid town. When I asked William what his friend used to do all day, he said something so shocking that I cannot remember it. We get very wicked in this bad country.

'But papa says there are superior people, of old Spanish families, "down South;" and William seems to think so too. I never saw anything like him. He says that real ladies *wash*—actually kneel down for hours together on little hard boards and wash their own linen; some funny people did so at Los Ojitos, a *Rancho* where he has been paying a visit. I do not think dear William is so unhappy as we feared. He leads such an active life, that, as he says, he has no time for romance and all that sort of thing. He is very kind to me, and calls me "little sister."

'William is writing to say Tommy must come out in the autumn. O, how I wish you were coming instead of that naughty little Tom! And papa is writing to congratulate Mr. Briggs and Edward. Kiss the pets for me, and write again soon to your ever-fond Clemmy.

'O dear! what a long letter I have written! I hope you will be able to read it. You may cross yours as much as you like.

'C. S.'

In the steamer which carried this letter to the

Isthmus of Panama, Don Guillermo Briggs, bearing with him the promise of abundant harvests, took passage for San Luiz Obispo, where he had a second interview with Don Bernardo. A strange reception awaited him at ' the little *Rancho.*'

CHAPTER VIII.

CRISTÓBAL'S FIRST BEAR.

BUT at Santa Perona, Carlo went up among the hills to a large glade of forty acres, girt about at its upper end by hoary oaks, and with clumps of *manzanito*, or red laurel, all about a rivulet that crept through slender grasses and wild flowers innumerable.

Here they determined to sow, the spot being near the head of the valley, and approached by a narrow gorge which would be easily guarded.

The first difficulty in cultivating any part of a *Rancho*, is to protect your own from your own. A Californian steer sniffing the breeze from juicy vegetables, or hearing the soft rustle of maize-leaves, will charge through a fence which seems impenetrable. A breach once made, in flows the myriad depredator, and a hundred acres are laid waste in a night. Then you gallop over and crush your sweetest pumpkins; a thousand melons shed their life-water at your horse's feet. You drive cattle over prostrate stems of maize, and when the foe is repulsed, have to acknowledge that victory is as costly as defeat.

The Franciscan monks used to build *adóbe* walls of

immense thickness and height round their gardens, as much to guard against this danger as to exclude the Indians of the Tulare plains. Water was conveyed from the hills in raised aqueducts, so that they could irrigate the ground in the dry season.

The chosen glade was a natural garden, as we have said. Its walls and aqueduct were nature's handiwork; a timber barrier to the stream would form a reservoir; and the soil was a fine soft mould many feet in depth. So Carlo set himself to make a harrow, that he might prepare the ground for seed against his friend's return. There was neither nail nor saw, awl nor gimlet, that Carlo knew of, within twenty leagues: but a harrow was a simple construction; and, with Cristóbal's help, he made one on the spot where it was required.

First they cut thirty-six pegs of *manzanito*, each twenty inches long, and bent them double. These they stuck into the ground in six equidistant rows, measured either way, and threaded them with six tough willow stems. Under these they placed six others transversely; binding them firmly at each intersection, and securing the double of the pegs. On the top they laid and bound other logs of greater weight. The bands of raw hide stiffen and contract in the sun; and the whole forms a respectable implement, which is soon fit for use.

Don Carlos, returning to the house with Cristóbal, found Manuel and Francisco in perturbation. The latter had been going his rounds to drive in the stragglers, when, hearing a lowing amongst the sand-hills, he followed the sound, and found a cow bewailing a mangled heifer. The tracks being through sand and light pulverised earth, had given no clue, except by their size, which induced him to follow them; but when they reached the more retentive soil in a hollow, the long foot-prints and the seams of five long nails in each left no doubt who the spoiler was.

Cristóbal was for hunting with the lasso, but Don Carlos objected. It would be madness to risk life on the cast of a lasso, and horses were cowards at the best. The *vaquéro* had seen great scars which a bear's claws had left on Carlo's thigh and stomach. He had no doubt of the *Inglés's* courage. They held a council in haste at sunset: a quantity of loose boughs were stripped off the roof of the sheds and bound on to a mule; Carlo and Cristóbal galloped off with spades and rifles, and had dug a hole seven or eight feet deep by the time Francisco brought up the mule and its load.

Then they laid their trap, covering the hole with leafy branches, these with earth and sand, and laying on the top the slaughtered heifer. Francisco withdrew with the mule and horses, and left these two lurking in the brushwood which overhung their trap.

It was poor shelter, a mere scrub of juniper, three feet in height, but gave them a clear prospect of what might come. Would the male bear (they thought) come alone to drag away the carcase, or would the dam and cubs come to the feast? The dam bears in

January ; the cubs would now be learning to forage.
If more than one bear came, it would go ill with them:
yet when Bruin came scuffling in sight alone, the relief was half a disappointment. 'If we'd only got
Will here,' thought Carlo.

The bear came along his old trail to the spot, saw
many tracks and the ground disturbed, looked up
through shaggy locks to where two heads appeared
above the scrub, and two bright spots glistened in the
starlight, looked down on the carcase, took one step
forward ; then an awful roar and a crashing of
branches drowned the simultaneous report of two
rifles, while the hunters drew their pieces in swiftly
and reloaded.

' *Es muérto, señor,*' said Cristóbal.

But now a loud snorting and shuffling dispelled the
illusion. The bear was working at his trench. Cristóbal's eyes flashed ; he wanted to rush down the
bank and shoot at close range ; but the other held
him with a firm grip. Carlo knew that at least one
ball had told, that the wound, and hard work, and
time, would fight for them. 'Keep cool,' he said,
'and lay your knife at hand : so.'

Presently the great head and neck appeared, heaving amongst the mass of sand : then the huge animal
emerged, wounded to the death, blind with dust and
fury, weak with toil and loss of blood : yet he looked
straight up the slope, and, with another roar, advanced.

But a spell was upon the half-caste : his glance was

along the barrel : his finger refused to move. 'Shoot first,' Carlo hissed, out of clenched teeth ; but in vain. It was a fearful moment. The bear was within ten paces, roaring, and advancing slowly. Then he staggered, stood erect, and fell, as a little puff of smoke rose from the clump of juniper. In the terrible eagerness of that moment, neither of them heard the report of the gun.

'Thy knife, man, thy knife!' said Carlo angrily, and snatched the rifle from Cristóbal's hand. The rifle was at half-cock.

But in a moment Cristóbal was on his knees by the dead bear, and had plunged his long blade twice into its heart. '*Ruéga por nosostros pecadores!*' he muttered in a deprecatory tone. 'A *vaquéro* cannot shoot.'

The next morning Manuel was sent with a mule to look after the dead ; and when the others returned from working in the 'glade of oaks,' at evening, he was still staking out the capacious hide, which measured six feet three inches in length by five feet six across, behind the fore legs.

The ingenious fellow had made a long bag of such parts of the heifer's hide as were available, and into this had poured a supply of genuine bear's grease ; not with a view to render the human hair ambrosial, but to anoint lassos, and for culinary purposes.

The head of a bear is considered a dainty by people of patriarchal appetites; and Carlo looked round with an air of profound melancholy, for it was not visible. But in the morning, while Francisco was milking, a savoury incense assailed the nostrils of Don Carlos, as the faithful Manuel uncovered a hole near the camp-fire, and triumphantly produced *la cabéza.* And while they are at breakfast, I will unfold the mystery of a trap-oven.

A round hole, two feet in diameter, is sunk to the depth of four feet. At the bottom of this a fire is kindled, fed with fuel for two hours, and allowed to subside into a carpet of hot embers. Upon this three large stones are dropped, and the head placed upon them, as on a dish. Over the cavity branches are then laid, and loose earth shovelled over these. So that the whole affair is not unlike the trap constructed for a living bear; except that it is smaller, hotter, and baited inside instead of out. It is also less dangerous to watch; and though the crisis of the larger one is more exciting, that of the smaller is not without pleasurable emotions.

CHAPTER IX.

RETRIBUTION.

CARLO was no longer the desponding young man who came southwards, in bitterness of heart, opprest with gloomy memories, and smarting from a recent loss. There was an improvident little maid, some twenty leagues away, by the wild sea-shore, who had wished to make him less unhappy, and had done so. That unhappiness, it is true, was not lost out of the world. By some inscrutable process she had taken the load, and was bearing it herself, as she had wished to do.

Certes there is a thread of mystery running through the woof of human affairs. Why should the hasty gift of love, which had been so pleasant to Carlo, be so painful to her? Had he done aught to deserve it? And was her generous impulse sin? I cannot see the right in either case.

Nor can I understand the infatuation of this young man. One has heard of love ruling 'the court, the camp, the grove,' though practical people accept that proposition with reserve; but that the same benign deity should govern the fortunes of Carlo, is opposed to the circumstances of the case.

A headstrong girl had offered him unasked affection. He had honourably repelled her advances, and returned her souvenir. They would not meet again. She would forget him, and he her. *Voilà tout !*

But perhaps the acquisition of the legacy served to encourage his delusion. He may have seen in the small sum the germ of great success. Waving seas of Indian corn, vines of muscatel, pear-tree groves, and luxuriant olive-yards, may have ripened in the summer of his dreams. The cattle on a thousand hills were his, and round him hovered, perchance, one sweet form of grace ineffable, more dear than all, the form of her who gave a value to all, without whom all were valueless.

It is fair to add that he did not expect this phantom-fortune to rise in a night. 'We will lay the foundation at once,' he thought; and worked and endured accordingly.

We pay heavily for experience, in cash, and in liabilities. It is well to make some use of the ' value received.' So Carlo, who had begun life with a determination to grasp happiness complete and indestructible at the outset; who had acted on this resolve with more spirit than discretion, and failed; now took her gently by the hem of her garment, and pointed to his work. And who shall say ? Perhaps she smiled and told him that it should not be in vain.

When I say ' to his work,' you must not confine my meaning to those few acres which the oxen had by this time traversed with the home-built harrow, nor to any amount of mountain-climbing, bear-killing, or manual labour performed in fifteen months. If you, for instance, are fairly engaged on the battle-field of life, and review any one week of your experience, and schedule what has proved your metal and tried you most, I think at the head of the list will stand the great negatives, and, in their turn, the small achievements, quickly dwindling to a point.

So it was with Carlo. What he had not done, that is to say, what he had refrained from doing, saying, and, which is much harder, from thinking, was part of that work to which he could point, not perhaps to you or to me; but in those moments when a man feels and resolves.

This is the appointed way to rest of heart: striving with the toiling surf and rolling waves which gird and overlie unfathomable depths of hope and trust.

It comes as a task to each of us: much painful effort, more or less misgiving and disappointment, go along with it: pleasure comes in slight instalments, enough perhaps to wet the parched lip, to save the eye from being glazed, the heart from being palsied; but the deep satisfying draught awaits us in the future; we pant and strive, but do not attain.

Carlo missed his friend very much in those days; but being more addicted to his own society than most men are at his time of life, and having real work on hand, as well as castle-building and the like, the time passed swiftly. He made Cristóbal, however, listen to his ballads; and that worthy, whose education had not taken a literary turn, heard them during the calm enjoyment of his evening *cigarito* beside the flaring camp-fire, and taught Don Carlos a villanous pronunciation of many words, and an intonation more rhythmical than pure.   Still the pupil was acquiring the language more like a Spaniard than a pedant; for the honest *vaquéro* was not behind the most lordly hidalgo in the use of figurative expressions and flowing periods of speech.

During his friend's absence, Carlo also composed a letter to Lord Saltum, being glad, in his solitude, to know that his guardian's oldest friend bore him good-will, and wished to hear of such an insignificant person as himself.

But the time for William's arrival drew near. Manuel and Francisco were despatched on horseback, with led mules, to meet Don Guillermo at San Luiz.

The cattle were now settling down to favourite pastures along the course of the stream, herding themselves in large bodies, as cattle will do when there is danger abroad.   It was only necessary to have a numbering every fourth day, and for one or other to ride round the valley twice daily.   The task became easier in two ways at once : the beasts having less wish to stray, and the men more knowledge of the country, and therefore greater ease in pursuing stragglers and recovering them.

Carlo is tilling in the ' glade of oaks,' Manuel and Francisco are on the road to San Luiz.   Cristóbal is going his rounds; he stops near the log-house which has been built for him, and thinks of wife and *mucha-chito*; and the poor *vaquéro* thinks he will be happy here. His wife is a warm-skinned, lissome Sonorian, and knows how to make a hovel happy, with the man of her heart. She is a tender wife and mother, and has little arts of gardening, which she has brought from her native land, and will have opportunity to practise here. And the lover-husband thinks how he would fain receive her with a gift: some linen sheets, and a woollen *sarapé*** of bright hues, or some cotton prints for dresses for herself and child.

When Cristóbal last visited the *Puéblo*, he drew a year's wages in advance. There, before buying what he should have bought for those who depended on him, he tempted his luck at *Monte* or at *Faro*, and lost the whole, coming back with a ragged saddle-cloth and downcast looks. And though the kind Señoritas have made poor Angela furtive presents, yet she has need of many things. And if she were not in need, what matters it? Who ever loved a woman without wishing to greet her kindly, and with offerings of love? Still the question murmurs in in Cristóbal's ear, '*Donde el oro?*' And the thought of that detested blood-money comes to answer, '*Quinientos pésos,* \$500;' and his hand droops to the

---

* A Mexican woven blanket, with a central hole for dropping it over the head (worn in which way it falls gracefully round the figure).

G

handle of the keen *cuchillo* ; and good thoughts have led to bad ones.

At this moment a voice breaks upon him, ' *'Ombre !* '

Is it the arch-fiend, or only one of the sprites of Michael Psellus ?

It is Costinetto, the Indian who brought the letters to Don Carlos, Cristóbal starts, and gazes at him in wonder.

The herdsmen of the Señor Don Joaquin and the retainers of Don Alberto know of the feud which exists between their lords. When they meet on the limits of the two estates, they pass each other in silence. But now the Indian speaks again,—

' *'Ombre !* your *caballáda* : is it missing ?'

Cristóbal is fascinated : ' *La caballáda ?* '

' Yes : I tell thee the brood mares of Don José are gone.'

' Gone ?'

' He has tracked them, and a large band of horses, in the direction of Lorenzo, and has gone with a body of armed men to occupy the pass, and has sent messengers forward to *El placer*, and heralds to the *Puéblos*, to call out the companies who have sworn to take the freebooter alive or dead : but'—and here Costinetto seizes Cristóbal by the arm, glares in his eyes, and grates out—' they are led astray by a false trail, a false trail, I say: *quieres oro, 'ombre ?* Wishest for gold, man ?'

Cristóbal draws the long bright blade out of his

gaiter-band, and makes a savage motion, as one who would stab an enemy to the heart: and so these two understand one another.

When men have a good purpose in common, it requires explanation, deliberation, and so forth; but when the devil is in two men's minds, they agree at a glance.

Costinetto leads his new ally round by a devious track to the southward, till they come upon a broad fresh trail, and unmistakeable signs that a large band of horses has recently passed, and is moving towards the defile of Chelone, a league to the south of Santa Perona.

How can they follow without help? There is no danger which either of these men would not face for gold; but even if they could secure their victim, they in turn would be surrounded and slain. But Don Carlos, *El Inglés*, is a valiant man, and a sure killer with the rifle. If he will go with them, they may prevail.

So, in the sultry afternoon, while Carlo, a votary of Ceres, not of Mars, was guiding the stubborn oxen in the glade of oaks, came the truculent *vaquéro*, and told him of the raid on San Pedro, how Don José had been misled, how the watchful Costinetto had found the trail, how the robbers might be over-taken in the pass and routed, the mares restored, and a large number of stolen horses rescued, and held for their lawful owners.

Overwhelmed with evidence, and with the rhetoric

·of Cristóbal, who poured forth his flowing tale, with copious verbiage and much gesticulation, Carlo gravely unyoked the oxen, hastened homeward for the trusty *pinto*, slung his rifle on his back, and got to horse without delay. But Cristóbal had to lasso fresh horses for himself and Costinetto; and the little delay gave Carlo time to feel that he might never return, and that William might find a desolate house. So he wrote another letter, 'probably my last,' he thought. It was written in pencil, on the fly-leaf of his *Romancéro*, and stuck up in the corridor. 'Dear Bill,' he wrote, 'there is no time for a pathetic letter, though if you find this on your return we shall be dead men. I am going with Cris. and another on the trail of Yankee Jim, who has made a raid on San Pedro. We don't know how many men he has. My fellows are as fierce as Salamanders, but they only carry the lasso. If Cris. comes back, give him $100. Take 100*l.* *yourself* to a certain person at L. O., and tell her what you know, and why I kept it dark. Whatever else I have is yours. Good-bye, dear, dear old friend.

'For ever yours,

'CARLO.'

And those three started in pursuit of a band, against whom Don José had raised the whole county, and some two hundred men were under arms.

They put their horses into a canter, and determined to quicken on the trail as fast as possible, so as to come up with the robbers before sunset.

Carlo sounded the Pedronian as they went. He found the right trail by accident, that morning; and, as all the best men at San Pedro had gone with the Señor, he came to Santa Perona for assistance. There is only the track of one shod horse,* that is *El Yanqué's.* There were two in his trail last year, but his comrade, 'Boccanegro,' was hanged in the *placer* in January. He probably has two or three *desperados* with him, and several Tulare braves. They will not betray him: no: he is *'ombre buéno* with the Indians; gives them horses and rifles, and has two wives among them. Yes, two wives. One is a Mexican girl, rescued from the Apaches, the other a Tulare squaw. If he reaches the Great Lake, he is safe. They will hide him and his horses in the mountain fastnesses, to the east, until pursuit is over: then the braves escort him northwards. Can they travel fast with so many horses? Two leagues an hour through the mountains, three in the plain. Yes, we are closing on them now: the trail is very fresh. Hist! what goes there?

Costinetto pointed among the trees on their left. Carlo saw a shadow gliding hither and thither. His rifle was unslung in a moment. *Crack!* 'It is only making the bark fly about; but concealment is of no use, now that *El Yanqué's* spies are watching us.

---

* It is quite possible to travel through Spanish California, from San José to San Diégo, without seeing the print of a horse-shoe.

We had better make a bold front.   The robbers will
think we are a skirmishing party, and that the main
body is coming up behind.'

The pious Cristóbal crosses himself.

' *Oro, oro*,' grates the other in his ear.

But the feeling has crept over Carlo that there is
something dreadful in dogging a fellow-creature to
the death in cold blood.   True, the man is a homi-
cide and a marauder; but it seems that he has
killed his men always in open fight, and often against
desperate odds.   Then that little touch about the
wives has melted Carlo.   He has a chivalrous regard for the thief, murderer, and bigamist.   He mis-
likes the idea of executing sentence upon him, unless
it so happen in fair fight.

Very different are the musings of the half-caste
and the native.   Cristóbal, as we saw above, is
craving money for an innocent end; but whatever
sin there is in covetousness possesses him wholly.
He has thrown himself headlong into one hateful
purpose; to take the blood of the freebooter.   He
fears him more, and regards him less, than a bear,
and would take him unawares.   True, the reward
would be paid if he were taken alive : but who could
bind *El Yanqué* ?   The man, alive, is equal to ten
other men.   Blood, blood !

The same desire, the same hate and dread of the
man, inspire both.   Costinetto is no longer young.
He is the same who, when living at the northern
limit of San Pedro, carried the Señora on his horse

to San Miguel, after she had been driven from her father's house. He loves the House of Buenaventura well; but he suffers from the gnawing disease which claims all the native Californians for its victims since the restraining hand of the missions has been removed: that disease is the love of play. *Oro, oro*; not the miser's gold, but the means of a few minutes, or a few hours, of delirious excitement, followed by the conscious luxury of utter abject destitution. This it was which made the brow of Costinetto dark, when he addressed Cristóbal by the log-house. When he found the double trail, he ought to have put spurs to his horse, and ridden at full speed to the gorges of San Lorenzo, and told his lord that he was wrong, but that if he sped through the pass before it was too late, and struck southwards, he would cross the robbers' track. But Costinetto had heard of the reward. The jingling of the coin rang in his ears; gold glittered before his eyes; his fingers quivered about the ever-ready knife; and turning up the left bank of the stream, he sought and found a kindred spirit for this ghastly enterprise.

And Yankee Jim, who, a few minutes before, felt secure from pursuit, and only threw out his Indian scouts as a natural precaution, heard the clear crack of a Kentucky rifle in his rear, thought that his double had been discovered by Don José, and that he had a large force close upon him. So he consulted his Indian guide as to the nature of the ground, for he had never tried the pass before, and gave his orders swiftly and like a great general, as nature had intended him to be.

He sent his skirmishers in advance, to line both sides of the approach to a narrow gorge, where he intended to make his stand and to fight. These had orders to wait until the rifles fired a volley, then to pour in a flight of arrows from either flank and pass off at the rear, waiting for orders. Fourteen Indians, on foot, swiftly disappeared, and took up the position indicated. One Mexican *bravo* and three Tulare braves remained with him. They drove the horses furiously along the pass, and, having reached the gorge, turned, unslung their rifles, and waited calmly, like men who know it is a death struggle, and that the battle is for the strong.

And Carlo came along, with his feeble force, reloading his rifle, but meditating mercy, and little thinking what a reception awaited him.

On his left the hill-side was swathed in a dense forest of oak; on the right flowed a deep, swift stream, with clumps of brushwood here and there among the rocks beyond. Carlo was riding in advance. He swept round a corner. Suddenly he saw, sixty yards ahead, in an angle of the pass, five men. one sitting erect in his saddle, with rifle in hand, the other four peering and aiming over their horses' backs.

He turned round at the sight, and shouted, 'Señor Don José! The enemy is in the gorge. Ride round, *por Dios*!'

Cristóbal and Costinetto hung back; they understood that it was a stratagem, and that they were
not wanted in front.

The robber hesitated for a moment. He did not
wish to throw away a whole volley and flight of
arrows upon that wretch on the piebald horse, while
a hundred men were swarming over the hill, to out-
flank his Indians and take him in the rear. So he
would not fire the signal, but shouted aloud, 'One
arrow for him, and follow !'

Whereat he fell off his horse, a dead man ; for
Carlo, seeing death and five armed men before him,
picked out the leader, and fired.

Now there was one thing which Carlo had neglected to teach the *pinto*, and that was to stand fire.
So, directly his piece went off, the horse swerved
suddenly round, an arrow whizzed past Carlo's head,
a bullet struck the *pinto* in the hinder quarters, at
which he plunged head foremost into the torrent,
amidst a shower of balls and arrows. The enemy
hurried away, to avoid the foe which they imagined
on their flank, and to get the *caballáda* out into the
plain.

If Carlo had ever so few armed men, they might
have now undertaken the pursuit, and rescued at
least a part of the horses ; but what could two poor
vaquéros, with long lassos and knives, do against
rifles and pistols in a narrow, winding pass ?

When Carlo reached shallow water, he tried to
catch the bridle with his right hand ; but his arm

hung heavily, and a great stream of blood, running down, poured off his hand.

The good horse struggled on to the bank, and stood by its master. Carlo felt himself growing giddy and feeble, so he called ' Cristóbal ! ' And that worthy came humbly down the bank, bound Carlo's arm with his long sash, assisted him to mount, ran and picked up the rifle, slung it on his own back, mounted, and turned silently back by the way they came. ' We cannot pursue them,' said Carlo.

' Since the Señor is wounded, no.'

And at that moment another horseman joined them. It was Costinetto, with a led horse, and something red across the saddle, which made Carlo shudder. He knew it was the body of the great robber. ' Two men, two men,' he muttered quaintly. ' God forgive me ! '

And as they wended homewards among the gaunt shadows which lay across their path in the moonlight, a fearful dirge followed in their wake. The *coyotes* were hunting on the blood-trail of ' Yankee Jim.'

CHAPTER X.

HESPER—PHOSPHOR.

THE passes of Chelone and San Lorenzo lead through the second arm of the Coast Range Mountains, eastward, into the great plains of Tulare ; that of Chelone from the southward of Santa Perona; that of San Lorenzo from the *Hacienda* of San Pedro.

The robbers had entered the latter pass, and followed it until they came to rocky ground, where the tracks would of necessity cease ; there they tied their whole convoy of mares and horses, tail by neck, in an Indian file, entered the channel of a stream which led them down again to the bed of the river, forded this and emerged in a moist hollow thronged with cattle, threaded their way through these across the moonlit plain, leaving only a single line of tracks, which would soon be confused by the numerous footprints of cattle crossing it, or filled up by the spongy nature of the soil. Having reached the sand-hills to the west, they relaxed the order, and their fresh trail had been discovered by Costinetto, as we have seen.

But the Don and his party following on through the rocky defile, hoping to recover the trail, were utterly foiled, and seeing that they were led astray, returned wrathfully to San Pedro. As they returned in the grey mist that rose from the river hollows before the rising of the sun, a *vaquéro*, leading a large black horse with a load across the saddle, met them. It was Costinetto with the body of 'Yankee Jim.' *

Great was the excitement in the county of San Luiz Obispo, and indeed in every Pueblo, mission, and Rancho, from San Diégo on the south to San Francisco on the north, as a thousand living witnesses can still attest. The great freebooter had fallen, ' *El Yanqué, El guëro maldito, El Demónio!* '

' *Valgá-me Dios!* ' ejaculated the *cabelléros.*

' *Ave María! Virgen purissima!* ' said the women.

For three years he had been the terror of the land. Those who fled from law and from vengeance joined him. The Indians of the plain were his scourge. With them he swept through the country, driving before him bands of horses, of brood mares, and priceless mules. So he threaded the defile of Tejon or San Lorenzo, sped northwards along the plain, skirted the river San Joaquin, and sold his plunder in the mining towns.

Once they had brought him to bay; and those who returned from that field told a horrible tale:

---

* As an historian I am bound to state that *El Yanqué* was *not* a citizen of the United States, but an Anglo-French Canadian, who had studied the traffic of horse-flesh in Texas and New Mexico.

how true or how false cannot be proved, but they brought back two dead men in a litter—a half-caste, and Juan, the son of Mariano Arianas.

On another occasion, *El Yanqué* had been surrounded when reconnoitring a *caballáda*, alone and afoot. He yielded to numbers, was taken to Monterey, and committed to prison for trial on the following day. But at sunrise on the following day two sailors swam ashore, and pointed to a small felucca that was standing out to sea. The astonished Alcalde and citizens saw a negro at the wheel, and the tall figure of *El Yanqué* calmly pacing the narrow deck. The *calaboose* was found roofless and tenantless.

But the mighty had fallen.

Nor had he fallen alone. *El Inglés*, the friend of Don Alberto, had been the mark for a score of arrows and half a score of rifles. Man and horse had been swept away by the mountain torrent. So the report had reached Los Ojitos.

Which *Inglés* was it? *El povrecito*, the poor little man without a beard. Where was Alberto? Not a word of him or of the other *Inglés*, *el guëro grande*, was heard. But Don Mariano took one man with him, and rode away beyond the hills, that he might learn the truth.

So it is, and so it will be. Men go their way, travel to and fro by land and sea, buy and sell, fight and are killed. The women stay at home, occupied about their little cares, and wonder and tremble at the chill blasts which reach them from the outer world.

I think that women who love suddenly and intensely are also smitten down at once by fierce strokes
of grief. They cannot take sorrow in instalments—
bear to-day what is sufficient for to-day, and reserve
the surplus for to-morrow.

It is so with Juanita. She needs to ask no questions, nor listen to any. Those swift balls and cruel
arrows have laid her low. It is Don Carlos who has
fallen. Can she not see him riding foremost in the
fray, and falling first? Has not the rushing of the
torrent sounded in her ears, since the tidings came,
a deadly downward flow, bearing in its wild course
the body of the man she loves?

Yes, *loves.* She will not give him up—will not
cease to love. She will go to him, and be with him
where he is. So she says to herself, poor child, little
thinking that Carlo, on his coarse canvas couch, is
tossing his fevered limbs, raving at intervals, and
calling her by all the tender names which haunt his
memory ; not dead, indeed, but far gone upon the
dim, shadowy road, and perhaps unconsciously clinging to life for her sake who would fain die for his.

The forty days of fasting and mourning are ended.
Easter has returned ; but gay colours are for gay
hearts, and Nita will have none of them. In the
sombre garb of Lent she moves listlessly about, with
drooping head, and bright hair falling round a pale
wan face. She does not seek to be alone, but rather
clings to Madre, who grieves to see her so calm and
tearless, present yet so far away. Solitude and vio-

lent bursts of grief come before comfort; but this
fear to be alone—this sad, silent wasting in the lap
of sympathy, is a grievous thing to look upon. A
half trance has fallen on her. When one speaks to
her, she starts and shudders, as if awaking out of a
horrible dream. Even Estéban pities her.

And Madre, to all around, maintained a calm demeanour, and looked as though hope lingered still.
But alone, she knelt and wept: 'My son and my
friend! O weary heart! Lost, lost! My God, Thy
ways are past finding out.'

One evening Juanita had lingered at her mother's
door, and heard this plaint. Then she came in, and
knelt too, and put one arm round her mother's neck,
and sobbed out, ' Dead, dead!'

Tears flowed at last, and her heart opened a little.
'Mother,' she said, pointing to her breast, 'he has
my cross.'

'I know it, sweet heart,' said the other.

'Think you he has it still, my mother ? '

'I believe it.'

'On his heart, there, where he is ? '

'I believe it well.'

Then they went and stood at the casement, and
gazed into the western sky, where Hesper shone
large and luminous. ' See,' Madre said thoughtfully,
' yon fair star now setting rises again before the sun.
Love encircles us ever. Trust in God.' And they
wept and wept, such blessed tears as rise in true
hearts only.

In the meantime William Briggs returned to 'the little *Rancho*,' and found the wasted form of Carlo stretched upon a pallet, with lack-lustre eyes and white fevered lips; the stooping figure of an Indian crone huddled in a corner, swaying to and fro, and muttering ancient incantations.

There was the strange letter as his friend had left it, calling to him, as it were, out of the jaws of death, and breathing of a double love, for himself and for the daughter of Arianas.

Carlo did not recognise his friend, but stared piteously at him, told him to ride round and take the enemy in the rear, that he was alone and outnumbered, that he could neither advance nor retreat; then, seeing William immoveable, he burst into a maniac laugh, and shouted, 'Blood, then, blood! Her brother fell. Who falls now? Fiend! Fiend! The wolf is on the trail. Who is this?'

His voice fell. His dim eyes still gazed at William fixedly. His breast heaved. 'Juanita!' he whispered, and, sitting up, stretched out his skinny arms, one bandaged, the other naked; 'Juanita! come nearer. One embrace! the—the first and last on earth!'

Then his head drooped on the rough wooden framework of the bed, his eyelids closed; and perhaps a tender vision succeeded the one of blood; for tears, 'idle tears,' again trickled out and fell upon the floor. It was hard for William to leave his friend; but the crone ordered him out. '*Vaya!*' she said, and pointed to the door imperiously. He felt that she was right, and went; so that the weird woman had Don Carlos to herself; and, as far as human arbitrement extends, his life was in her hands.

Who was she ? Costinetto had brought her, and a mule laden with oranges and tomatos and febrifugal herbs, from the estate of San Pedro. She was his sister. Housekeeper, nurse, and doctor to the old Señor Don Joaquin.

William then put his strong shoulder to the wheel. Leaving Manuel to assist La Forina, and to bring him word if she wanted him, he took Cristóbal and Francisco, and laid down his seed, and swept it over with a large bush of boughs, and built a lodge at the head of the glade, where Francisco might live and become a terror to crows.

Then came the Señor Don Mariano, on his roan horse, with Diégo in attendance. Don Carlos was still alive, or half alive ; *Gracias a Dios!* The avenger of blood lived to receive a father's thanks. La Forina tried another experiment. Don Carlos should see him, should see HER father. Carlo looked at him with a puzzled air. The Señor came and took his hand—a lean, sallow hand. The other seemed to make an effort of memory. '*El pinto*,' he said, sadly, and fell back, exhausted by the effort.

Where was Alberto ? Mariano asked of William. Then William told him everything : how two hundred cows were already gone ; how Alberto had not spent a week on his Rancho ; how it was in the market with

H

two hundred more cows for $10,000, or less; how
Don Carlos had received a legacy of $2,000, part of
which had been invested in seed, in implements of
agriculture, and in swine. But William abstained
from mentioning that he thought of purchasing the
little Rancho himself, or indeed that he was possessed
of funds adequate to such an emergency.

William said that the Señor Don Silvestro Starchie
had a client who was willing to purchase, but that
they thought it right to offer Don Mariano the re-
fusal, nor would they take advantage of the impru-
dence of Don Alberto by hastily closing with the
offer.

'Alberto is imprudent: *Ca-ramba!* but if he must
sell, ten thousand piastres is a fair price. Money is
scarce in the metropolis. The drain of gold continual; the import of coin small. No; for me, my
Rancho and my spot of land in the Pueblo are sufficient.'

The hidalgo went on to say that it was a little
Rancho, but a pretty one, and with fair pastures,
that he should be loth to remove his cattle.

William observed that the intending purchaser had
offered to keep Don Mariano's cattle, without commission, and that, as he (William) and Don Carlos
were to remain in charge, every care would be taken
of them.

'The *caballéro* is good; but I shall press upon him
a fifth of the increase of my stock. Why should a
man buy land and give the grass?'

Nor did William allude to his friend's passion for the hidalgo's daughter. The subject was a closed book between them.

After three days of anxiety, La Forina pronounced that Don Carlos was out of danger. He saw and recognised Don Mariano in a feeble manner; but had lost all recollection of what had happened from the moment when he wrote, and fastened up in the corridor, the farewell etter to his friend.

So the lord of Los Ojitos went his way; but before he went he addressed William as '*Mi compadre Don Guillermo.*' To appreciate the extent of this favour, we must understand that the manners of the Señor were stately and reserved.

We have not recorded many of his words, partly because he is not a principal actor in our little drama, partly because it is impossible to render Spanish talk in the garb of English talk, but principally because he spoke little. His was a generous nature, restrained by habitual caution—a quality which perhaps he valued more highly since the annexation of his country by the United States.

In attempting to move with his time, the lord of Los Ojitos was under heavy disadvantages. In the first place, his title-deeds to the *Hacienda*, as he well knew, were doubtful. Whereas the Franciscan Order could show the original Royal grant to the whole domain, his was only a tenant-right, to become freehold on certain conditions, the fulfilment of which would now be difficult to prove or disprove; but the worst feature in his case was that this right had been obtained from a short-lived Government, all whose acts had been repudiated by its successor, before the American war had broken out. Truly the United States Commissioners had a perplexing task, in this, as in many other cases of disputed Mexican titles.

Again, Don Mariano, like most of his countrymen, though admiring the energy and enterprise of *Los Yanqués,* had little respect for their other personal qualities, and not being able to converse freely with them, was unable to discern their real sentiments, and the relative merits of one and another. In the meantime he studied the rudiments of their language; cultivated fruit at his little estate of Las Rosas; drove his two-year-old steers to the northern markets; and invested his capital in shares of the great Agua Fria Mining Company.

As William said on a former occasion, there was method in his generosity. He saw in the two *Ingléses* useful allies; and now especially, since one of them had avenged his cause, had a personal regard for them. They were men after his own heart; brave, gentle, and of simple tastes.

The dry season in that region lasts from April till October without intermission. Then the pastures on the seaboard fail; the beasts fall off and are unfit for market.

But by keeping a thousand head or so at Santa

Perona, in good condition during the summer drought, he might sell each year at an advantageous moment, and net double profits.

So the Señor called William his '*compadre*;' he admired their sheds, approved of the glade, praised their vigilance, was amused at the idea of turning acorns into pigs' flesh, took an affecting leave of Don Carlos, and was prodigal of kind phrases. Moreover, he left Diégo behind, who, as he said, was a bad *vaquéro* but a good gardener, having learned that craft under Don Gabriel, his mayordomo, at the little garden in Los Angeles.

' 'Wonder whether the old boy will come round,' mused William as he rode away.

'*Son Caballéros estos hombres*, those are gentlemen,' mused the other as he rode away. 'One loves my child, but will not speak. He has killed my enemy. I love him, *pero no le conoco, Ca-ramba*! I do not *know* him.'

And, indeed, what paterfamilias would willingly hand his only child over to an interesting stranger in a ragged shirt? Your hand, Don Mariano; *nous sommes d'accord.*

Let us return to Los Ojitos. It is eventide. The Señor has arrived, dismounted, greeted wife and sisters; but his daughter receives him with a pallid face and vacant stare. Then her secret opens upon him, for he has brought the clue to it from beyond the hills. So he calls his wife aside; they talk earnestly together for awhile; then the hidalgo comes up to his child and kisses her, and passes out to attend to other matters.

But Madre puts her arm round Juanita's waist, leads her to her own room, and says tenderly, 'Take off this sad garb, my child. Don Carlos is alive and recovering from his wound.'

No one else was present at the scene, nor is any detailed account of it on record. He should be a bold man who would attempt to fathom the ocean of a woman's heart in its depths of joy or sorrow. I cannot do it. I am only informed that as the sun sank below the horizon, the young lady came down stairs in a white frock; that her colour had returned, but that her eyelids were red and swollen; that she told Julia she was 'so happy,' and then burst out crying again, which must be considered a curious illustration of felicity.

In the still moonlight, Juanita trips round to the cottages at the back of the house. Angela, the Sonorian, was sitting sadly in the corridor, listening to the distant moaning of the sea.

'Don't rise, Angela,' said the other, smiling through her tears; 'I bring you good tidings. Cristóbal is safe and well, and has a house built of trees on a beautiful knoll near a river; and you and Thomasito are to go and live there and be happy all the rest of your lives.'

And she tripped away again. The waves ceased

to moan. The moonlight was sunlight. Juanita was a gay butterfly sporting in its ray.

And Angela was right in connecting her with the sunshine. Some women's hearts, and perhaps some of ours too, in the spring-time of youth, are like lenses which catch a few rays, however faint and pale, and concentrate them into one bright luminary, in the light of which they see—well, perhaps some simple object upon which the heart is set, some fond imagining or sweet illusion.

Nor may we intrude on the private intercourse of the hidalgo and his wife. Recounting the fray between Don Carlos and the robbers, as he had received it from Cristóbal, the father must have reopened a deep wound which time had closed, but which always bleeds internally in a mother's heart. Probably the renewed pang brought a little access of tenderness to the father's heart; and whether the mother took that occasion to plead a certain suit is not recorded. Her manner revealed nothing. She was an instance of the still water which runs deep; calm but profound, gentle yet strong; strong in endurance, in faith, in love.

CHAPTER XI.

CURSORY.

DON CARLOS recovered from his wound; but pale
Death, which had alighted for a moment in the
mountain defile, and hovered for many days round the
humble dwelling at Santa Perona, took wing to San
Pedro, and there beat so loudly at the door that the
proud hidalgo was fain to open, and to send post
haste to San Miguel for the monk.

La Forina returned to her duty, and this time her
answer was not of life, but of death. The Señor
would not live many days. Often had the Fray Don
Antonio besought him to forgive his daughter. Now,
in the face of the death-summons which La Forina
pronounced, the spiritual father stood beside the
father after the flesh, and said, 'My son, it is well to
be angry, but it is better to forgive.'

And the time had come when a man should exercise the quality to which he trusts; so a messenger
was despatched to Los Ojitos, conveying an apology
from the Señor Don Joaquin to the Señor Arianas,
and begging him to bring his wife and daughter, that
the old man might bless them before he died. And

they came in time. A wound which had bled for so many years was healed; but the Señor Don Joaquin passed away.

By the end of March William and his men had sown twenty acres with barley and twenty acres with maize, dividing the 'glade of oaks' equally between the two. Carlo took up his quarters at the head of the glade as soon as his friend would suffer it. There he grew strong again in brain and limb, cunning in device against the crows, skilled in all approaches to the glade, so that any track of steer from the valley, or of bear or wolf from the mountains, was noticed by his watchful eye, and prompted measures to restrain or to avenge. At the upper end of the glade the barley grew and ripened, stiffened into dusty gold, and fell before the sickle; while beyond that arose the tall forest of Indian corn, bowing heavy tasselated heads, and waving its green plumage in the breeze.

Angela proved a guardian angel to the swine; while Cristóbal became a gardener. The whole venture of beans, tomatos, onions, pumpkins, and melons, was intrusted to his wife and him, with Diégo as a supernumerary; and as the Señores allowed him to pay for a share of the seeds, out of certain money which Don Carlos had given him, the *vaquéro* recognised in himself an agriculturist who had an interest at stake as well as a service to perform.

As soon as the period of close mourning for his father was ended, Don José rode over to see the

Englishmen, concerning whom he had heard so much
from Don Silvestro, from La Forina, and from Costinetto. This was about the middle of April. Carlo
had to thank the hidalgo for the services of the skilful nurse who had set his arm and tended him through
the fever; but no services which the house of Buenaventura could render would repay the obligation under
which Don Carlos had placed them by exposing his
life in the pursuit of their enemy. Every *Ranchéro*
in the country owed him a debt. 'And for me, I owe
you a *manáda*,' said the Don, whose forty mares had
escaped from the Indians, and came straggling
through the pass of San Lorenzo, within forty hours
of the time when *El Yanqué* fell.

Don Mariano, he told them, had gone to see the
working of the Agua Fria mine, in which he was interested; but the Señora and her daughter and Doña
Julia were staying with him, and sent their greeting,
and thanked them for a handsome present of books
which had come to Los Ojitos, and hoped a long
time would not elapse before they should see the
caballéros. There were other friends of theirs, at
least of Don Guillermo, coming before the maize
harvest, and an evening ride should not separate old
friends.

Don Carlos had not quite recovered his strength at
that time, and was very busy during the day, so that
he could not avail himself of Don José's kindness at
present.

William Briggs, however, went and came, and

went and came, and well the good chesnut knew the
trail to and from the mansion of Don José ; but very
rarely Carlo rode beside his friend, and never past the
lodge of Cristóbal, where he would stay and exchange
a few kind words with Angela and her little swine-
herd (for Thomasito had been promoted to that office),
and then would return to his solitude among the oak-
trees.

A constant interchange of services went on between
San Pedro and Santa Perona, much to the advantage
of the female saint or her clients. For instance, Don
José would want the assistance of William and one
or two herdsmen for a day's work, after which they
would fare sumptuously, and return laden with
gifts to Santa Perona. Then Don José and half a
dozen Pedronians would come over and help the
Englishmen with some work. At sunset the Don
would send his men home to their *Ranchería* ; would
take his tea and *carne secco* with his hosts, or, if he
was in luck, a stew and a mess of beans ; would smoke
and talk long over the camp-fire, and return alone
when the moon was high.

On these occasions Don Carlos was of the party,
though on other nights he would stay alone in his
glade. ' I can't go there, you know, Will,' he used
to say ; ' at least I won't, though the *pinto* pulls hard
when· he gets to the boundary. Go along, *donec
virenti canities abest* ; I like the rustle of the maize
leaves, and the chatter of the green frog on the banks
of my stream.'

Sometimes William would stroll up with him, or to him, of an evening, and try to talk him out of his sadness; but Carlo's silence 'stumped' him, as I find it written in his diary. Indeed, to take up your parable, and talk to a dear friend who is smoking a long wooden pipe, and staring into the fire, wholly unconscious of your eloquence, *is* disheartening.

The frequent evening visits of Don Guillermo to the *Hacienda* may be attributed to this solitary and reserved habit of his friend, with whose musings over that lonely fire I could fill a book; but it would be a melancholy book, and perhaps a wearisome one: not that Carlo was without hope or without energy; for have I not said that he grew sound of brain and limb, skilled and cunning in his pursuits?

But after a hard day's work, or a fatiguing day's sport, when a man sits over a lonely fire, and consumes the fragrant weed, not hopeless, but with hope postponed indefinitely, combating a strong temptation with a stronger will, yet with an effort that leaves him weak; I say if a man so sits, and listens to the sad whisper of a breeze in rank foliage, or a scanty rivulet's tinkle in the pale moonlight, his thoughts are apt to take a melancholy turn, or at best to have a pleasure of that subtle kind which does not appear to others; a touch perhaps of what is called 'the luxury of sorrow.'

On one occasion Don José had come with his Indians to construct a sunk fence, with a *palizáda* against the upright side, round Cristóbal's garden.

After all the poles had been cut and pointed for the palisade, the fence occupied ten days. It formed three sides of a rectangle, and might be flooded from the river, which formed the fourth side.

On the last day the Señoritas rode down from San Pedro, one of them at least with a beating heart, to see the garden turned into an island; but Don Carlos did not join the party, although he had been at work there every day for hours, and indeed had designed the fence; he was busy that morning in another direction.

At length it occurred to Don José that Carlo avoided meeting the ladies. One evening, after supper, he turned suddenly on William, and said to him in English, 'Why is it that your friend comes not? I also would have him for a friend. Tell me why he stands aloof?' And William said, 'Ask the Señora.'

So he turned less abruptly to Madre, and said, in Spanish, 'Tell me, my sister, why Don Carlos will not come to my house. His friend refers me to you.'

And Madre turned to Juanita, who was standing by her side, but looking down, and blushing behind a veil of golden hair. She put her hair aside and kissed her forehead, and said quietly, 'The fault is not ours.'

Then the truth flashed upon Don José. 'Ah! my benign one,' he said, curiously. Then, thinking of it for a few moments, he added aloud, 'The *Inglés* is

poor, is he ? and proud as a *caballéro* should be, however poor. Shouldest have loved a rich man, *muchacha. Valga-me Dios!* A poor *caballéro*, and a maid
with ten thousand cows to her dower ! *Que carajo!*
What a dilemma !

And from that time forth he set himself to devise
how the thing might be managed, took Juanita
under his wing, cultivated Don Carlos more kindly
than before, was always genial and merry with his
new friend, continually renewed his invitation, and
yet would make excuses for the other, when he
refused : ' Yes, I see, we could not expect you tonight ; you are fatigued. So. This fever pulls one
down, and leaves the desire to be alone. *Adios, amigo!
Hásta mañana !* '

A man of superior education and vigorous mind,
Don José formed, as it were, a link between the old
and numerically small race of *Ranchéros* and the ' hungry people ' which swarmed over the Sierra Nevada,
lighting first upon the gold-fields, but soon to spread,
and even now spreading, far and wide over the land,
to till, to sow, reap, and gather into barns, and to
count their dollars by tens of thousands in a year,
where their predecessors had counted them by thousands in a decade.

Carlo and the Don became confidential on the subject of deer-stalking and the prospect of a lion-hunt.
They projected much sport for the autumn, when the
crops should be gathered in, and Don José would run
down from his senatorial duties in the capital, to ex-

patiate in the broad plains of Tulare, or thread the gorges of the Sierra del Monte Diablo.

Now, too, Carlo heard the story of a lion* hunt which took place in the previous autumn. The beast had been brought to bay, and while the *vaquéros* were making their cast, a certain horse turned and fled. A moment, and the lion was in pursuit. In vain they pressed their horses. Pursued and pursuer vanished swiftly. At length they came upon a prostrate horse. It had broken its leg in a squirrel's hole. A few yards farther on lay the body of a man with a shapeless gory mass on its shoulders. It was poor Jacinto, a kinsman of La Forina. Carlo expressed a desire to make the acquaintance of that Puma; but Don José shook his head, and said reflectively, '*Ca-ramba!* but the devil was a fierce one.'

Now and again, when the Señor was going over to 'the little Rancho,' Juanita would mount her horse and gallop by his side till they reached the boundary house, where she would dismount and wait with Angela till he returned.

'So kind and thoughtful he is,' Angela would say, meaning, whom do you think? And she would point to her clean white sheets and cotton prints, and say that *he* ordered them to be paid for out of his own money, though he had no sheets for himself, but slept on a common hide; and gave this warm bear-skin to Thomasito, because, as he said, the bear might have

* Felis concolor, Puma.

killed him, and then he should have wanted no robes; but Don Carlos killed the bear; my *hombre* only stabbed it afterwards.'   A confused narrative: women are so discursive.

Those interviews were very pleasant to Juanita. A young lady of delicate nurture, and accustomed to the society of refined minds, forgot herself so far as to spend hours and hours with a mere Sonorian half-caste, the wife of a common *vaquéro*!

But, after all, it is a world of burthens. The earth bears its load of humanity and heavy brutes; these bear our burthens or pay the penalty of premature death.   So we must each stagger along, if we are weak, with our seen or unseen load; and a helping hand or an arm to lean upon sometimes does not come amiss when we have to clamber among rocks, or toil through sand, or wander to and fro in darkness.

So it happened that this frail damsel, whom Angela had likened to a butterfly, had a weight upon her heart which the gauzy wings could barely lift; and if another could share that burthen, or give her little draughts of strength to bear it, could she complain because that other owned a taint of blood, or that her husband was a herdsman?   Sympathy is a want of nature, not of breeding.

And then a gallop of two leagues along an undulating plain, through sunny pastures and dark, silent groves, with a flash of the bright river here and there; to inhale the balmy breath of cows, and the fragrance of the summer wind, laden with perfume from flowery knolls and the dim retreats of scented herbs; this is so pleasant to the young. And what damsel would not love to ride such a gallant steed by the side of such a splendid uncle?

Now, although I have shown in glimpses the heroic side of Juanita's character; and though I think that out of nature's book she had learnt some of the nobler lessons of life, such as depth of purpose and strength of trustfulness; I am not to exalt such acquirements unduly, or forget that children should obey.

When last we accompanied the paternal Arianas on horseback, we saw black Care sitting on his crupper, and dinning in his ears that Don Carlos, who had killed his enemy, loved his daughter. '*Ca-ramba!*' rejoined the Don, 'but I do not *know* Don Carlos.' And is it to be expected that a man should pass a lifetime in growing rich, should find himself past the meridian of life with one child only, should have his ear wedded to certain forms of speech and modulations of the voice, his sympathies educated, as it were, on a certain type of mind and heart, with all its good and its evil; and should suddenly cast sympathies and prejudices to the wind, and bestow his wealth and his child on a stranger?

The Don went so far as to think about it; but he loved his countrymen with their virtues and their vices, their drawling bastard-Spanish and olive complexions; he loved his garden in the Pueblo, his *Rancho* on the wild sea-shore, his grape-vines, and his countless herds; but, above all, he loved his child. It was too much to expect of a father's heart. '*Valga-me Dios !*' he muttered. '*No quiero los estrangéros.*' Not that he really was without regard for his new friends, but that he was not ready to make such a terrible venture, or to sacrifice so much.

Still the father saw there was danger. He saw into his daughter's heart, and knew that hot blood coursed in her veins though her skin was fair. He knew that the calm waters of her life, though smiling in sunshine like a mountain lake, might be lashed into fury by a sudden blast, seethe around the little bark of duty, and bury it in a living tomb. He felt so much, and loved her the better for being like her sire. 'A woman's tender hand,' he thought, 'shall guide the helm.'

So he said nothing, but was more gentle to his child than had been his wont. But Doña Juana again took her daughter aside, and said, ' We must conquer this unwise passion, my child.'

But the other looked at her calmly. The child was a woman in the face of danger.

' Do not tell me love is foolish, mother. This is a new lesson from you.'

' Love is wise when wisely placed.'

'On a brave man and an honourable, as my father has said.'

'Your father forbids. It is unwise to disobey.'

'O, cruel father! Did you not disobey for him?'

'And the years of sorrow I have passed!'

'Have we not been happy, then?'

'Happy in each other, child; but I have hidden a bleeding heart from you. My cup of woe is full to the dregs. My father and son are taken, now my husband and child will love me no more.'

And an expression of anguish came over the Señora's face, which was wont to beam with faith and trust. The other was overcome. Who was she, to shatter the building of a life, to destroy her mother's peace?

'*Madre mia!* I will never leave thee, never give thee pain. Kiss me, dear mother. Now, tell me: what shall I do?'

'My lot is cruel. I must strike what I would cherish.'

'No, no; only let me love him. Papa shall not see it: I shall be so uncomplaining.'

And so the dialogue ended. The mother had made the attempt and failed. *Fiat justitia!* Juanita has been weighed in the balance and found wanting. Alas, for filial obedience under the sun!

And who shall say how much of this blind trust was founded in delusion?. Had Juanita known that Don Carlos had returned the amber cross, think you hope could have struggled on, or love lived without hope ?   Had Madre known it, would she have failed in her attempt so easily ?   Of one thing I am well assured : that they little thought the pious pledge of love was reposing amongst *cigaritos* and German tinder in the *chaquéta* pocket of Don Alberto.

CHAPTER XII.

EPISTOLARY.

THE editor of this narrative has at hand an original document which casts a light upon some of its characters in a new group, and some of its incidents from a new point of view; and as it is written in that engaging style known as the female epistolary, he does not hesitate to transcribe the greater part of it for the reader's edification. It appears that Don Alberto with his young wife, and Don Silvestro Starchie with his amiable sister and daughter, arrived at San Pedro early in June.

'My darling Annie' (the latter young lady writes), 'a thousand thanks for your nice long letter, which has given me I can't tell you how much pleasure—

*　　　*　　　*　　　*　　　*

'Auntie and I have been here for a fortnight. Papa was with us for the first few days, but was obliged to go back to San Francisco, and will not return till the maize harvest, which will be in the latter part of July. I should perhaps have told you about the other ladies first. There is Doña Juana (or Madre), Don José's sister, who ran away with her husband, the Señor Don Mariano, years ago, and was never allowed to come home till quite lately, when the dear old gentleman was dying. Her daughter is a lovely pet: we call her "Nita" or "Niña." Then there is Madre's sister-in-law the Doña Julia, and Doña Isabel the wife of Don Alberto. The only gentlemen at present are Don Alberto, who is Madre's brother-in-law, and the Señor Don José, our host.

'Now, dear, I know what you are waiting for. Yes, William comes very often, and is such a favourite with everybody. He is not sad, I assure you; indeed, he says "Carlo does the romance part of the business" for both of them, and William is growing very wicked. Take this, for instance.

'Last night, after supper, Don José had been telling us a terrible story of a lion-hunt, when Nita said, "Dear uncle, how I should like *un leoncillo* (a little whelp)!' The Señor only smiled; but when we were standing by the fountain afterwards, La Forina, an old Indian nurse, came and touched Nita's hand, and said, "Dost indeed wish for a whelp?" Nita looked at her for a moment, then clasped her hands and said, "O, no, Forina, dear! Don't ask him!"

'I told William, who was here at breakfast; for I was afraid La Forina was going to ask him to get a cub, and the lion is a terrible creature; and poor Jacinto, a *vaquéro*, was killed by one last year. But William said, "It's Carlo. He's *épris* of his old nurse, and would fight the foul fiend for a word from her lips." But La Forina is very old and ugly; and only think of William talking like that!

'But before I tell you anything more about him or anyone else, I ought to give you some idea of this most romantic spot. The house, then, forms three sides of a square, with a double piazza (*el balcón*) running round the inside. The doors and windows of both stories open on to the piazza, which opens on to a smooth lawn with a few pear-trees and the most delicious fountain. Beyond the lawn and the broad valley, the chain of the Monte Diablo rises in tall peaks, over which the sun rises, and at sunset they seem to faint away in an amber-tinted sky.

'You must know that Don José speaks English beautifully, as if he were reading out of a book; and so I told him that the Casa of San Pedro reminded me of a poem which I am very fond of, though I don't understand it a bit; and I repeated to him the stanza—

> Full of long sounding corridors it was,
> 　That over-vaulted grateful gloom,
> Thro' which, the livelong day, my soul did pass,
> 　Well pleased, from room to room.

'He made me say it again slowly; then, "*Virgen purissima!*" he exclaimed, though I can't see what the Virgin Mary has to do with it—can you, dear?

'The weather is intensely hot. I am writing at a little low table in the piazza. The ladies are sitting about working; at least, Doña Isabel is pricking her

husband with a long needle, and Juanita is peeping
over my elbow. She is something like my Annie,
with real golden hair, not yellow like mine, and blue
eyes. The Señor says that the type is hereditary in
his family, and that it appears in every second or
third generation. As for Don Alberto, he looks at
us two together and says, " *Guëras, guëras, y tan
bonitas !* " How fair they are, and how pretty! But
you know, dear, some people's looks are more com-
plimentary than others' words.

' To return : in the first place, there are no carpets
in the house except a little scrap in each bedroom
under a crucifix ! Only think, dear ! but the boards
are kept clean and white like the deck of a ship.
There are no damask curtains ; but the glass doors
and windows have little muslin blinds to them. The
doors are left open all day and the windows all night,
though it is quite cold just before sunrise. In the
daytime we lounge about on little ottomans covered
with crimson satin, in the cool corridors—I mean
the ladies when I say "we." The gentlemen seldom
sit down. William says chairs are a relic of the
dark ages. They lean against the cedar pillars, or
lie down on the smooth floor, which makes them look
very interesting. You know we like to have gentlemen at our feet, dear. But William says that Don
Alberto looks like a tame *iguána*, which I believe is
a species of crocodile.

' The domestic servants are wives and children of
Indian *vaquéros*, men who gallop about after cattle,

flourishing long lassos or *reátas* over their heads. They live in the back part of one wing, and have a court at the back, where the cooking, washing, and other things are done. The ladies don't "wash" here, I am happy to say.

'But half a mile from the house is the *Ranchería*, or village, containing about fifty families of peöns, or tame Indians. It is such a bizarre place. Fancy a double row of brown sugar-loaf huts, each eight feet high, and fires burning day and night along the middle of the street. Then imagine a number of brown women, with long black hair escaping from a yellow silk handkerchief bound round the head, with little white chemises and a short skirt of printed calico. Set these to work stirring porridge over the fires, or pounding maize, or plaiting rush baskets, with a host of little boys fetching and carrying, or nursing babies, and you have a sketch of the *Ranchería*, when the men are absent. Those funny creatures pop their heads through a hole in a woollen *sarapé*, which falls around them in broad stripes of white and crimson. It must be a very uncomfortable way of dressing, but they seem to like it.

'And what *do* you think, dear? Don José has offered Don Carlos ("Carlo") something very handsome to come and live here and be his overseer. The Indians are idle when he goes to San José to take his seat in the Senate; and one or two have learnt to gamble and drink, and will corrupt the others if care is not taken.—June 17th. I was going to tell you more about Don Carlos, but we went for a long ride yesterday, and I cannot write in the evenings, for we are all together, talking, and singing, and sighing, or perhaps laughing, in the piazza, without any lights but the moon and stars.   It is only in the morning, when the gentlemen are not here, or only Don Alberto, that I can write.   And now this dear Julia wants to know what I can have to say after writing such a long letter, and whether you are beautiful, and whether I think you would like her, which I know you would.

'Now, Annie, I am going to tell you two secrets. First, I think Juanita is almost or quite in love with William.   There is evidently something preying upon her mind.   She is very sad and restless ; but when William comes in, will go and cling to his arm, and look so loving, and say pretty, simple things to him : but he is so calm and impassive, that of course one can be more free with him than with anyone else.   Indeed, he treats her and me too as if we were children !   If he did condescend to fall in love again, I think it would be with Julia.   She is a brunette, with large lustrous black eyes and downcast lids, and the most beautiful mouth.   She scarcely ever smiles, though her teeth are *perfect* ; but, when he speaks to her, lifts up her eyelids and looks calmly at him, or goes on with her work, sustaining her part in the conversation by a little softly-spoken word here and there. Between you and me, I don't think she has much to say for herself ; but she has a way of sighing when he is near her, *which looks like something*; and he certainly is more gracious to her and to Madre than to any of us.

' And I am opprest with another secret which is no secret to you, namely, that William has bought "the little Rancho" and two hundred cows with his own money. All the others here, except Auntie, think that a merchant in San Francisco has bought the estate, and that William is his bailiff. And I am sure I shall let it out some day to Nita, who twines herself round one in the most irresistible manner, and asks questions in broken English with such a sweet smile that one can't help answering her. Only she never asks questions about "Don Carlos."

' What shall I or can I tell you about him? He will not come near us, nor does he even live with William, but all by himself in a solitary glen at the head of this long valley. He cannot be so wicked as we thought, or William would not be so attached to him; and I heard Don José say to papa, "No, I do not *like* Don Carlos. It is a man whom I love." Doña Julia, who saw so much of him at Los Ojitos, says he is a slender person, not much taller than papa, but with curly hair, grey eyes, with a mild expression and long dark lashes like her own. And then she gives such a sigh and says she wishes he were a rich man, which puzzles me, because I cannot make out whether she is in love with him or with William.

' I heard the praises of Don Carlos again, at the boundary of the two estates, from a gardener's wife, who showed me the hide of a most dreadful "grizzly bear" which he had killed. I told you in my last the fearful story of his fight with the robbers in the pass of Chelone. And only yesterday William told us that he had a wrestle with a she-bear in the gold mines, you know, dear, or whatever that place was at the foot of Mount Shasta, and that they both (Carlo and the bear) rolled down a hill together and tumbled into a dry ravine, but that Carlo got up and ran away while the bear was rubbing its back! I should so like to see him!

'Perhaps the real secret of his popularity is that he is generous to poor people. He refused the reward for killing that bad man, and gave two hundred dollars of his own to each of the *vaquéros* who were with him (though I believe they hid behind a rock), and two hundred to La Forina, who nursed him through the fever.

'But I must not forget to tell you about threshing the barley, which we arrived just in time to see. The rick is in the middle of a round enclosure; and a number of wild mares with their colts, except the very little ones, are driven in. The Señor, and William (Don Guillermo they call him), and several Indians, stand on the rick and pitch the barley down behind the horses, which keeps them in perpetual terror: so they go galloping round and round for hours together, only stopping now and then to take breath and stare wildly about them, and then off again. In the middle of the day they are released, the straw is thrown over the palings and the corn collected with wooden spades. Fresh mares are then sent for, and in the meantime we have dinner round a real camp-fire, under a great sycamore-tree near the river, with the wild figures in their red and white *sarapés* hovering about.

'The mares are splendid creatures. They are never ridden, you know, but wander about in a large band called a *manáda*, with one horse and their dear little foals. We have beautiful horses to ride, too. They never want to trot, and the least touch of the rein on the neck guides them wherever you want to go.

'Now, my dear Annie, you will be tired of your poor little gossiping Clem; but—

*   *   *   *   *   *

'Next month you shall hear about the maize harvest, which I am longing to see; only we shall have to go so soon afterwards. Two pretty sisters of Isabel are coming here on a visit before the party breaks up. I wonder whether they will make an impression upon anybody?

'William is writing by this mail. Kiss the pets for their dear Clem, and kiss this paper which I am kissing now, that our lips may meet across the wide, wide sea.'

CHAPTER XIII.

SUMMARY.

Ay cuán mal, dulce enemíga,
Las veras de amor me pagas!
Pues, en cámbio del, me ofréces
Ingratitud y mudánza!

'DO you know, Will,' said Carlo to his friend one evening, 'I think I could stand it better if I were to see her now and then.'

The ladies had been three months on the next Rancho, and Carlo had not yet set eyes upon them.

W. B. I think so too.   I'm not for total abstinence in anything.

C. Can you tell me one thing?

W. B. I'll try.

C. Is she sad?

W. B. No, I can't say she is.

C. Another thing, Bill; does she wear a little amber cross, which you must have seen her with, at Los Ojitos?

W. B. No.

C. Never?

W. B. Never.

Then Carlo thought to himself—'After all, I'm a fool to make a mountain of a molehill. If she ·loved me, she would wear the cross, and wouldn't be so jolly. I know I'm not. I should like to see her happy. I'll go. No, my heart fails. I'll stop here with my frogs and snakes.'

W. B. And there is another thing, Carlo.

C. Out with it.

W. B. You won't be furious.

C. No, I'm past that.

W. B. Well, I think; mind you, I don't know, but I think—— In short, there is a very handsome young man paying a visit to San Pedro just now.

C. Yes?

W. B. A sort of cousin; that is, son of Mariano's cousin, who was Director Suprémo of the Republic.

C. I heard Alberto talk about him. Shot, wasn't he?

W. B. Yes. Well, this Marcos is his son.

C. Exactly.

W. B. And, you know, the ex-director invested his gleanings in British Three-and-a-Quarters.

C. Downy old gentleman.

W. B. So that Marcos has the advantage of you.

C. Yes, I see. Then there's no occasion to stay away any longer.

And they rode together.

We have seen in a former chapter how Clem had been led, by the artful ways of a certain Señorita, to think that her affections were fixed on William.

William, on the contrary, thought to himself, 'They love to feel their power, these pretty tyrants. She knows Carlo is afraid of her by his staying away. She is coaxing me to bring him, that she may keep him at her feet.'

William's keen eye had also noticed that Juanita did not wear the cross which Carlo had returned. He had seen that token peeping from the folds of Carlo's shirt, on their arrival at Santa Perona, and missed it after Alberto's second departure.

'She has thrown it aside, in a pet,' he thought, 'and will bring him to an account the next time he comes within range of her guns.'

So William was not sorry to see Carlo stay away from this wily foe for a time. 'Yet,' he thought, 'there should be a limit to evasion. When the enemy is fairly baffled, and one's magazine replenished, one should face about and show fight.'

On these general maxims, William had latterly been anxious to take Carlo to San Pedro ; and since the arrival of Don Marcos, he thought all danger was past. 'Enemy's right wing engaged : no chance for her.'

So Don Carlos was marching on to victory.

At the Casa there was a numerous and a pleasant, if not merry, gathering. Don Mariano had returned with his kinsman. The two beautiful sisters of Doña Isabel had arrived, and Don Silvester Starchie had returned in time for the maize harvest.

They were enjoying the cool hour and the reflected

light of sunset : for the great house stood on the slope of low hills which bound the valley to the west; the court, with its trees and fountain, were in deep shadow ; over the valley hung a purple haze, above which the peaks of San Lorenzo * stood up, black and rugged, against an amber sky.

William was right in his conjecture, as far as the gentleman was concerned. Don Marcos was a suitor for his little cousin's hand. He had told her, this ten years, that he would marry her, whether she would or no ; and to such an arrangement there seemed no possible objection.

He had also the advantage of Don Carlos in other respects. He was at least four inches taller than the latter. Like the Señor Don José, he had black luminous eyes and magnificent purple moustachios. He had, moreover, an estate as large as half a county, in the province of Sonora, reported to contain vast mineral wealth. His yacht, a Baltimore clipper of two hundred tons burthen, was riding at anchor in the Bay of Monterey ; and he was a shareholder and an active manager of the great Agua Fria Mining Company.

This brilliant personage, leaning against a pillar of the corridor, opposite to where Juanita sat, sang a *cancioncito*, to which he accompanied himself on the guitar. It ran thus :—

* A precipitous group in the chain of the Monte Diablo.

Hast thou forgotten
    Thine ancient vow?
Wilt thou recall it?
    Recall it now.
Others have told me,
    Come, tell me thou;
Hast thou forgotten
    Thine ancient vow?

Others have told me,
    Come, let me hear;
Put thy sweet lips, love,
    Close to mine ear;
Tell it not sadly,
    No, not a tear;
Grief cometh gladly
    If thou art near.

Are thine arms round me
    Tenderly now?
Hath a spell bound me,
    Or is it thou?
If it be thou, love,
    Come, tell me now;
Hast thou forgotten
    Thine ancient vow?

Obviously the song might mean much, little, or nothing. Any value which bystanders or sitters attached to it would depend on theories for which it was not responsible.

Juanita listened calmly enough to the first two and a half stanzas; then her ears refused their office; the blood rushed to her finger-tips, suffused her face in the dim twilight, rushed back to her heart, and stagnated, or seemed to stagnate, there.

For her eyes had lit upon two figures that stood near her, waiting for a pause. Don Guillermo was one. She had scarcely seen the other. There was no need of seeing. His presence was felt in every nerve of her delicate frame. It was Don Carlos.

'He comes thus,' she thought, 'to taunt me. He holds my token, and has kept apart all these weary months; and now, thinking I love this man, has come to triumph over me.'

And when he drew near, she rose up, with the blue blood of her mother's house overbearing the woman in her heart. She looked him coldly in the face: her lips smiled scornfully. '*Como le va Usted, Señor Don Carlos?*' she asked politely; and receiving no answer, went on: 'The ladies will be charmed to know a *caballéro* of whom they have heard so much, and seen so little.'

And taking the arm of Don Marcos, she swept a curtsey to Carlo, stepped out on to the lawn, and vanished among the pear-trees.

Carlo, too, was shocked at heart. 'I lifted her from the ground,' he thought. 'I would not bind her: I bound myself at her feet, and she tramples on me.'

Carlo had greeted no one. Alone in his wretchedness, he stood there, stunned and senseless, for some minutes.

'*Aquel hombre!*' said one, in wonder.

'*Tan povrecito!*' said another, who thought him crazed.

K 2

But Julia, like a white angel in a dim aisle, walked up to him tenderly.

' Don Carlos,' she said, in a soft low tone.

He looked at her with a weird scared glance, glided behind a pillar, sped along the lawn, flew over the low railings, and vanished.

William followed him. The Señor Don José followed William round to the sheds. The ladies followed as far as the wicket-gate.

' What harm, Carlo ? ' asked William innocently.

' Harm ? ' shouted the other. And again Carlo made use of the strong monosyllable; but this time with a harsh sound of compressed rage. His eyes glared at William under the dark shed, as he swept past; striking the *pinto's* flanks with the great blunt rowels of his jingling spurs, and going at the rail fence which closed the yard; crashing through the two top bars went the wild horse, and away again, past the astonished company, who saw Don Carlos vanishing in this way, without lifting his *sombréro*, or saying a word.

'*Ave María !* ' they whispered: ' *Aquel hombre !* ' ' *Aquel Inglés !* ' ' *Virgen Sanctissima !* '

But the *sángre azúl* resumed its course in Juanita's veins; her heart spoke up and would be heard. ' Hast been cruel,' it said to her; ' art worthless, to trample on a brave man, bound to thy feet.'

Don José passed the matter off lightly. Don Carlos had lived so secluded a life since the fever. He was liable to a seizure in company. He would

come again. The oddness would wear off. *Es náda,*
—it is nothing.

The company resumed their positions. Conversation went on again in that desultory capricious manner suited to the occasion. William returned, and
having seen that the Doña Julia alone made a kind
advance to his friend, when staggered by an unkind
blow, he took her hand and said to her,

'God bless you! *Dios te guarde de mal!'*

She lifted her eyes and looked into his honest
heart, and, no doubt, saw it as it was; while he felt
how different was the ray of this calm tranquil
flame from the old-love light, with its fitful gleams
and flashes.

William, you see, was forming a Platonic friendship for Julia.

But Nita sat apart, with downcast eye and tremulous foot, nor looked up into the starry heavens or
to the 'everlasting hills' for strength, but rebelled
against nature, and belied her heart.

' Why did he come at that moment ? ' she thought.
' Why did Don Guillermo bring him ? Cruel, heart-
less man! Would not bring him once in these long
lonely months; and now tells him I love another,
and brings him to see it.' And she beat the ground
with an angry foot. Still this was a shade nearer
the truth. It was William, not Don Carlos, who
timed the visit.

Again one smote the guitar; but she rose hurriedly
and slid away in the gloom of the corridor. If any-

one had looked, he would have seen another white
figure in pursuit; two ghosts flitting noiselessly
along.   So true it is that we are surrounded by a
legion of spirits, and that we move not alone, whether
we move for evil or for good.

They sped along the corridors, reached the wicket,
glided through without a sound, crossed the broad
road, and vanished among the standard fruit-trees.
The moon was below the hill; only a few dim starlight glimmers reached them.   The first spirit felt
itself clasped by the second.   It turned and said,

' Comest to taunt me ? '

Julia. When have I said an unkind word, Niña ?

Nita. Why come, then, seeing I wish to be alone ?

Julia. We are alone together.   Unburthen your
heart to me.

Nita. Where shall I begin ?

Julia. The cross: where is it ?

Nita.   He has it still.

Julia. Then he loves you still.   It is plain enough
on other showing.   Think you Don Marcos would
be so crushed by your feeble scorn ?   Knowest well
he would mock thy mock-majesty with a laugh.   Be
content, *hermanita* ;   hast the whole heart of an
honourable man.   'Tis a gem of price.

And Juanita went back comforted, with her arm
round Julia's waist; not content as the other would
have had her, yet feeling that the gem of price was
hers.   And possession is something, if not everything.

Have a care, my pretty maid! What we value lightly we hold loosely. It may escape your hold yet; and in its place you may find the Señor Don Marcos, with his estate, and his yacht, and his Agua Fria shares, and his heart in his own keeping. *Quedado!*

Let us return to Don Carlos. Arrived at the glade, restored by the cool night air, he thought, ' I have made a fool of myself, and exposed my folly.' Then pride came to his aid. ' Enough of this,' he thought; ' three months' blind folly and superstition, worshipping a figment of the brain, a molten image fused in the furnace of the heart.'

Having stalled the *pinto*, and examined and oiled the scars which that noble steed had acquired in charging the oak rails, Carlo loaded his pipe, put his pot on the fire, and went to his canister for tea. ' I'm a lord of the creation at last,' he mused ; ' such a blow as that knocks a fool down, and he gets up a man.'

Three days after these events there was a merry scene in the 'Glade of Oaks.' Twenty-five Pedronian women, in the picturesque costume described by Clem, were marching through the maize, trampling down each stem, and plucking out the golden ears. After them straddled swarthy, unclad children, placing rush baskets to catch the falling treasures, and emptying these in rows of glittering pyramids.

The glade rung with other voices and other

laughter than that of the squaws, at their pretty toil. For in Carlo's bower was a picnic party of the gayest. It consisted of all the ladies and all the gentlemen from San Pedro.

Don Carlos had shaken off his weird humour, had been to and fro between San Pedro and the glade, had become a universal favourite, and, indeed, with the help of Don José, had organised this scene of rustic dissipation at the ladies' special request. They longed to see the hermitage : it must be ravishing, the hermit was such a strange, interesting person !

Now the tiny rivulet sparkled in the midst of the glen, and the great oaks stood sentinel around. The lodge was newly thatched with green rushes from the great lagoons: the floor had been levelled and swept, and overlaid with Chinese matting. There was Bordeaux wine, there were juicy melons, maize cakes, and *cigaritos*.

No horses were admitted within the charmed circle that day. They were left at the sheds below ; and the ladies made the ascent leaning on the arms of the *caballéros*.

Nita toiled up the ravine on the arm of Don Marcos ; and Clem tripped gaily in front of them, escorted by Don Carlos.

The Señor Don Marcos, with Alberto's assistance, had prescribed and mixed a pungent little dose, calculated to relieve his cousin of the last symptom of her heart-complaint. He was therefore pleased to be gracious. ' *Don Carlos es muy caballéro*,' he observed to the patient. And finding occasion to address Carlo during the ascent, he invoked him familiarly as ' *Compañéro*,' or ' *Amigo*.'

And as they climbed, Carlo saw his amber cross, that token to part with which had cost him sighs and groans and tears, at the end of a dainty little chain on Clem's bosom. His self-scorn kindled at the sight. His heart, or something in its place, bounded wildly. 'Gave it away to the first comer,' he thought; O fool! fool! to pour one's self out in weakness at such feet.'

And if Juanita had treated him with scorn on the night of his first visit to San Pedro, he shared that feeling with her now. He had been a fool, an ass, an idiot; so at least he said, and perhaps thought that he meant it.

Nita, by-and-by, saw the cross there too, and sickened at the sight, and called Julia aside and directed her attention to it. But Julia said it was ' another cross.'

' I tell you it is mine,' said Nita, and thought despairingly within herself, ' How shall I get me away to a convent, and hide my head from these brazen lies, and this hot burning shame ? ' And she hated Don Marcos, hated Don Guillermo, and as for Don Carlos and Clem, her eyes withered at the sight of them. What a heart was hers to take out of the world and offer it alone to her Maker !

Late that evening, when they were about to leave the glade, William suddenly left Julia's side and ranged himself by Clem, while Carlo found himself escorting the Doña Julia.

Somehow or other he could not feign in the presence of this young lady alone. His spirits flagged. Beautiful and gentle as she was, he wished her 'anywhere.' He had no mind to be serious.

'Forgive me, Don Carlos,' she said to him, 'I wish to say something.'

'The sound of your voice will heal the smart of your words,' he said. 'Say on.'

Julia. The cross?

Here Julia's wrist felt Carlo's heart throbbing furiously.

C. As you say, Señora; the cross?

Julia. Gave you it to the *Señorita Inglésa?*

Carlo thought that Juanita had deceived her. He burst into a loud harsh laugh; and those in front turned round to look, and those behind whispered, '*Valga-me Dios,*' for there was a strangeness about the scene; and the reputation of Don Carlos, though brilliant, was shrouded in mystery.

They were picking their way down the narrow defile. The sun had already set. Huge trees spread their branches across the rocky way, shutting out what little light there was above. Julia returned to the charge: 'Answer me, Don Carlos, if you love the truth.'

'You trifle with me,' he said angrily.

She was not offended, but closed her other hand round his arm, and leant more of her light weight upon him. 'There is some mystery,' she thought; 'he is true.'

And by this little act of confidence Carlo was overcome. He hurried on, so as to distance those behind. 'Señorita,' he said softly, 'I am not myself. I think you can tell what it is to love with the whole heart. I did it, and my heart is broken.'

She clung closer to his arm. 'Yet tell me what you know about the cross, my friend.'

'*I* cannot tell you. Ask *HER*.'

So the mystery remained unsolved.

CHAPTER XIV.

A CAST FOR A LIFE.

———— And make the libbard sterne
Leave roaring, when in rage she for revenge did earne.

THE festivities which took place in the Glade of
Oaks, on the last day of gathering the maize,
were succeeded by a long, sultry, solitary day, which
Carlo whiled away in the harmless but monotonous
pastime of shooting crows.

Those marauders eyed, from the neighbouring
oaks, the glittering piles of maize, eyed askance the
watchful sentry, and occasionally told off a foraging
party to make a descent on some outlying stores.
These detachments suffered severely in killed and
wounded, while the survivors made but little impression on Carlo's commissariat.

The surface of Carlo's mind was altogether occupied with repelling these attacks, and inflicting these
losses; but in its depths lay the emptiness of an
abiding loss, and the wreck of an assault that had
laid the citadel in ashes.

When the sun had set, and the crows had retired
to roost, Carlo piled wood on the fire, less for warmth

than company, drew a bottle of cool Bordeaux out
of the stream (it was a relic of yesterday's fête),
poured half of it into his pannikin, and drank.

'Love is gone,' he mused, 'but something worse is
left. I will not keep it. It shall all go together;
so help me One who is stronger than I !

'Yet she is terribly beautiful. All night she
stands before me, soulless, yet warm and life-like.
All day she dogs my footsteps. She meets me at
every turn. She kneels before me in the dark shed,
or sweeps her wanton curtsey in the dim corridor.
I will go and look at her once more. I will try to
forgive her; and there an end. Have I not learnt
to suffer? Fool that I was—*Nescius auræ fallacis.*'

That evening there was an Indian festival in a
wood near the *Ranchería* of San Pedro. It was a
sort of harvest-home gathering, and its chief charac-
teristic was the lineal descendant of a war-dance,
but now performed in honour of Ceres.

Carlo led the piebald horse down the dark ravine.
He felt like a man going on a guilty errand: for he
was doing violence to his reason, which told him
either to avoid the cruel one altogether, or to brave
it out like a man, and continue to meet her face to
face, and learn to hear her voice and see her smile
unmoved.

'Yet,' he thought, 'I should like to see her, unseen. She cannot be all herself before me. She
dreads me, and perchance hates me. I would see
her enjoying the present, and forgetting what is past;

so I, too, might learn to forget. Only fancy her de-
ceiving Julia about the cross. *I* give it to the *Señorita Inglésa* ! Ha! ha!'

And again Carlo shouted the loud harsh laugh.
The horse drew back in alarm. This was not its
master's voice. Carlo patted its neck, and led on
over the spot where Julia had asked him that cruel
question. Then he continued in a bantering tone,
but with caresses, 'Wilt do the like, *pinto mio*, that
knowest all my humours? Wilt take another lord
and master, and revile the old, *pinto mudable*, change-
ful particoloured horse ?'

And, having now reached the valley, Carlo leapt
into the saddle; and the good horse, pleased at so
much confidence, tossed its proud head, and would
have lashed Carlo's legs with its tail, in ecstasy; but
that member was of the order denominated 'rat,'
and had not been endowed with superfluous plumage.

As they rushed past the boundary lodge, Cristóbal
shouted 'Señor! Señor Don Carlos !' But he spurred
on, deaf to entreaty, till the boundary was far behind, and the great house in view.

Then he turned out of the beaten track, and
followed a path which wound among the trees.
Before him the glimmer of distant fires flashed
among the hoary stems. Presently a glade appeared. At one end a rim of dark figures, flecked
with gaudy tints, encircled fires, above which rose a
tall pole crowned with a sheaf of maize. At the
other end were the party of Don José.

A low hum encircled the glade, swelled into a loud murmur, which rose and fell, came nearer, and died off in the distance, with a mysterious effect, for the singers were concealed in the woods. At certain points in the choric song, the whole circle round the fires, the old men, the women, and children, burst out with ' Avooo—voo,' a grand diapason.

Then came the dancers, flying over the dark rim of seated figures, leaping and pirouetting among the fires and round the trophy, with extravagant gestures, while an outer circle hovered round the sitters, and fluttered in and out among the trees, till the stately forest oaks seemed to reel and stagger in the fitful light.

A pause ensued. The gay party drew nearer to see the pipe go round, and to hear the strange people making merry ; but Julia and Juanita remained where they were.

Juanita's eyes became fascinated by something she saw, or thought she saw, in the dark grove. First a pair of eyes fixed on hers ; then, as her sight grew accustomed to the darkness, the figure of a man on horseback, rapt and motionless. Julia's eyes followed hers, and saw the same vision. It was Don Carlos—his ghost, on a ghostly horse.

' I have killed the man I love,' thought Juanita ; and in presence of that solemn ghost pride forsook her, mistrust forsook her ; tears streamed down her face ; she stood weeping, with clasped hands, as who should say, ' Thou wert true. See the truth to which mortal eyes were blind. I loved thee. All else was nought.'

But, in truth, it was Don Carlos in the flesh; neither did he move at all until figures coming between hid her from his sight, until the choral murmur and the dance began again, and he could retire without the sound of his horse's feet among the twigs and acorns being heard.

After him, as he went, there glided a dark shadow, stooping and turning as though it feared detection. It was La Forina, Carlo's quondam nurse and confidante.

'What is it, mother?' he asked.

L. F. Speak low. You love her still?

C. Yes.

L. F. Her heart is breaking.

C. What can I do?

L. F. Tell her of your love.

C. It must not be. I will go and die.

The other looked at him, as if she would search out some wild corner of his brain. Carlo stooped towards her.

'Dost fear death?' she whispered.

C. No, good mother.

L. F. Wilt seek the lioness in her lair?

C. Ay.

L. F. Go then. Domingo is on the trail. Cristóbal is ready. And hark ye, *carillo*—the Señorita wishes for a whelp. If thou comest again, bring one in thy arms.

Again the *pinto* vanished swiftly; but La Forina lingered, shadow-like, among the shadows.

At length the games were ended. Real night came to Juanita—silence, solitude, and sleep. Then she dreamed of that apparition which she had seen under the oak-trees; but it appeared to stand outside the enclosure at Los Ojitos, waving her a last farewell; and in her ears resounded the solemn thunder of the ocean, as it had done that night when her friend had ridden away.

Early in the morning La Forina came to her. A red ear of maize lay on the little table in her room.

'What is this?' said the old woman, in scorn.

J. A red ear.

L. F. And why?

J. I gathered it.

L. F. But why keep it?

J. I cannot tell.

L. F. Dost want emblems of a new love? Will not the old suffice?

J. Throw it away. I want no emblems, nor any love.

L. F. Not if the old be true?

J. It is too late.

L. F. And honourable?

J. You speak the truth.

L. F. It may not be too late yet.

J. How? too late? too late?

L. F. He may return.

J. From whence? Speak.

L. F. Ay, let me speak. Thou wouldst have proofs of love—wishedst for the whelp of a lioness. Don Carlos is in the mountain on thy quest; one from which men sometimes do not return.

La Forina had been opening the door in the meanwhile, and now slipped out, leaving Juanita quaking with fear, not unmixed with pleasure. This was some tangible danger, not the nameless dread of last night. Now the vision of Don Carlos comforted her. His spirit was watching her; she had clothed it with his form, and had even figured to herself the faithful horse. He would not perish. Our Lady gave him so much grace. And she turned her face to the pillow, and prayed with all her strength to *nuestra Señora de los Remedios.*

On the former evening, while the rooks were going to roost on their watch-towers round the Glade of Oaks, and Carlo was saddling the *pinto*, that he might go and take a last look at Juanita, a lioness * was ranging in search of prey for her cubs; a splendid beast, swift, strong, and crafty. To the keen ears came, amongst other sounds, the distant sound of Carlo's pigs. When Thomasito brought his charge home, one was missing. The theft was at first attributed to *coyotes*; but no trace of blood could be found near the ford ;† the squeaking which they had heard a while ago must have misled them.

* In Spanish '*leona*,' the female Puma.
† *Coyotes* devour their prey at once.

At this moment a certain mongrel, named Domingo, lifted up his voice, and uttered a dismal
howl, leered round at his master, wagged his tail,
and walked into the running water. Finding nothing
there, he swam across, worked up and down the bank,
hit the trail, gave tongue again, went along a few
yards, and then stood still, howling piteously, with
outstretched neck and tail.

Cristóbal, being on foot, would have recalled the
dog—

'Domingo! Domingo!'

'You-ou-ou-ou! Youyou! You-ou-ou-ou!' was all
the answer he could get. So he returned to the
lodge, where Angela and La Forina were in conclave,
and told them of Domingo's strange behaviour.

The wary old woman mounted her mule, crossed
the ford, and examined the trail. It was that of a
lioness. The male will not hunt till night; the dam
only when foraging for her young. Its lair must be
far distant; the choice of a pig instead of a colt or
calf showed that.

Just then Don Carlos rushed past at full speed.
Cristóbal, as we read, hailed him in vain. But now
La Forina would go on and send him back. In the
meantime, Cristóbal could ride to the Glade of Oaks,
and bring the good rifle which had killed *El Yanqué*,
and could load his short brass gun, and see that the
flint was clean and sharp; they should also prepare
a sumpter-mule with the great saddle-bags; for Don
Carlos would kill the lioness and bring home the cubs.

Poor Angela sat and trembled. Of all names since the death of Yankee Jim, *la leona* sounded most terrible in her ears. She thought an evil spirit had assumed the form of La Forina, and come to lure her *'ombre* to destruction.

As the old woman was taking her departure, she beckoned Cristóbal—

'What horse wilt ride?' she asked.

'*El Negro*, the horse of *El Yanqué*; 'twill not swerve.'

'*Buéno*; and if the trail be warm, wait till daylight. Fail not.'

Cristóbal went and made ready; that is, he brought the good Kentucky from the Glade of Oaks, he fed the great black horse on barley, saddled a sumpter-mule, examined the flint and priming of his gun; but, more particularly, with true *vaquéro* instinct, he prepared his stoutest saddle-girth, eight inches broad, of forty horse-hair twists—he strained and oiled his longest lasso, fitted for a cast of twenty yards, and put a keener edge to the long *cuchillo*.

These things Cristóbal did by the pale starlight, and by the rising moon; but La Forina reached Don Pedro, found Don Carlos in the forest, and sent him off on the perilous quest, as we have seen; so that he arrived at the ford just as Cristóbal's preparations were complete.

It was now late. The moon was up. Domingo lay whining dolorously; for the puma had nigh three hours' start, and the scent was growing cold.

But Don Carlos arrived in high glee. To a brain racked with emotion, the prospect of excitement, of danger, was intoxicating. He laughed at Angela's rueful countenance. ' Shalt have a *leoncillo*, too, my pretty Angela, fear not.'

The jingling of their spurs and the murmur of their voices died away. And another woman lay at home praying for the absent.

The pedigree of Domingo was complex; his dam being a Cuban bloodhound, his sire a mongrel Californian greyhound. Malgré the bend sinister, he was a true dog, both of nose and eye. No sooner did the horsemen come across the ford than he took up the trail eagerly. It led them a league across the plain, then swept to the north-west, skirting the estate of San Pedro and the mountains for three leagues more.

In the pass of San Lorenzo the ground became rocky and uneven. Now they were in a large valley, which appeared to be a basin in the surrounding wall of rock, only cleft and traversed by the channel of a mountain stream. Huge boulders lay disorderly about the level, and round their bases sand and gravel, drifted by the torrent, which, during the rains, would overflow its narrow bed.

Here the scent failed. Domingo cast about in vain, now lost behind a boulder, now flitting across an open space, at length coming back to its master, baffled and weary. They debated what should be done. Cristóbal thought the beast must have doubled down the watercourse and regained the plain. Carlo dismounted : here and there were little banks of smooth sand, among which the now meagre rivulet wound its way ; and clear shallow pools occurred at intervals ; he examined these as they glistened in the bright moonlight, but could find no trace.

As they stood in consultation, a deep bay from behind made them start. Carlo sprang into his saddle. Again it came from a dark corner of the glen, followed by a mighty roar, at which the *pinto* trembled, and angry echoes went rolling up the pass. Dismounting again, Carlo unslung his rifle, and advanced. Cristóbal remembered the words of La Forina, 'Wait till daylight ;' but now it was too late, so he followed, on the black horse.

'Keep back a little,' Carlo said ; 'be ready for a cast when she springs. Is the hand steady ? One look back as he spoke, a cheery look of confidence. Cristóbal threw the brass carbine on the sand, shook the coils of his lasso loosely in the left hand, and poised the noose with his right. Carlo turned, picked up the carbine, and advanced again.

The position from which he wished to draw the foe was a natural chasm in the side of the mountain, defended in front by a cluster of rocks, and lying within a dark line of shadow. He moved quickly forward to the edge of the shadow, and called 'Domingo !' The dog was among the rocks, twenty yards in front, and answered with a friendly howl, but did not retire.

Carlo sat down, and gazed intently. After a few seconds the dark surface of a rock seemed to move; then came a stifled cry, and, instead of the hind legs and tail of Domingo, Carlo saw the glare of two green eyes and the grinning of white tusks, so he called aloud, 'Are you ready?' raised the rifle on to his knee slowly, steadied the silver sight between the two green eyes, and drew the trigger.

The hammer came down with a hollow sound on the damp cap. With dismay Cristóbal saw him lay the rifle down, and stand bolt upright, taking aim with the brass carbine, but retreating slowly, step for step, as the enemy advanced.

Cristóbal sat like a rock on the great black horse. 'Keep your eye on her,' the other said; 'my trust is in you. As soon as she staggers, make your cast.'

The puma's tawny mass was now half in shadow, half in moonlight, moving stealthily, with crouching form and restless tail. Fire and smoke burst from the brass mouth of the carbine, and a roar of fury answered to its bark.

Firm and dauntless stood the black horse. Cristóbal poised his noose aloft; and even while the growl was dying on the puma's angry lips, and her strong back arching for a spring, the fatal coil was drawn tightly round her throat, and she felt herself dragged irresistibly from her course. For Cristóbal, having made his cast, wheeled about, dashed his spurs into *El Negro*, and the horse was tugging at its load.

Carlo's heart leapt within him. 'Straight, straight,'

he shouted, ' from the chasm, as you love your life ; ' for the puma was holding back with might and main; but if Cristóbal had worked round towards her stronghold, she would have let the lasso slacken, and sprung upon him in an instant.

Then Carlo turned, picked up his rifle, put on another cap, and ran after them. The struggle was a fierce one. They had not dragged the puma far when Carlo came close upon her left flank. Again he shouted, ' Let go your lasso, and wheel round to the left.' Cristóbal's thigh was nearly bursting with the strain across it. He obeyed at once.

The infuriated beast turned too, and found itself face to face with Carlo—calm and cool was the latter, mad with rage the former.

Once more she gathered her mighty force together for a spring, lashing her flanks with angry tail, and uttering a low, deep growl; but right through her brain sped the messenger of death; a darkness fell upon her; down she lay, gasping helplessly; and a purple stream of blood gushed from between her glazing eyes.

Cristóbal, hearing the report of the rifle, wheeled again, and, seeing what had happened, dismounted, crossing himself piously, and muttering a prayer of thanks.

As these two stood over the quivering carcase, their hearts warmed within them. Carlo extended his hand, across the body, to Cristóbal, and wrung the other's with a nervous grip, saying in an unknown tongue, ' God bless you, my hearty ! '

Life is always sweet ; as those who have risked it on a percussion cap, or the cast of a lasso, or a die, can attest ; and well Carlo knew that but for a tight collar which encircled the puma's neck at a critical moment, the Fray Don Antonio would have had to bury the bare bones of a heretic in the sacred precincts of Saint Michael.

CHAPTER XV.

QUEST AND REQUEST.

WE left Juanita lying in bed, and praying to Our Lady of Succour for Carlo's safety. She was startled from this exercise by the thunder of a Chinese gong. It boomed through the 'long-sounding corridors;' it wailed and moaned in distant chambers; it throbbed and palpitated in Juanita's heart. Was it his death-note? 'No, no! Pity! Succour! *Madre de Dios!*' And again she prayed, and forgot that the chocolate was waxing cold, and Don Marcos wrathful.

For that day was the high day of some obscure saint whom Don Marcos delighted to honour; and he, with his *compadre* Don Alberto, was about to escort a party of ladies to the mission of San Miguel, that they might avail themselves of certain spiritual privileges at that shrine.

Then came Clem, to rouse the loiterer, whom she found praying instead of sleeping. Juanita said to her, 'Tell Don Marcos I cannot go. I am tired, sick, faint. And come here, *mi hermana.*' So Clem came near, and Nita twined a little dimity-clad arm round her neck, and kissed her once, twice, thrice; then took the amber cross which still hung on Clem's bosom, and kissed that too, and looked so prettily at Clem, and said, ' It ‾is well. I have forgiven him. Wilt stay with thy little sister to-day ?' So Clem performed the appropriate osculations, and said she would stay too : what did *she* care about Saint Blank?

And she ran away to tell Don Marcos that La Niña was faint, and would stay and pray at home, and she with her : that they should both be ready to dance and sing in the evening, at the festivities which Don José was preparing at home.

Clem was puzzled at Juanita's interest in the amber cross, which bijou Clem had found, neatly folded in tissue paper, on the table in her room. It was accompanied by a card, on which was written her name, subscribed by the initials J. J. Having admired a similar ornament worn by Doña Juana, she concluded that her host, the Señor Don José Joaquin de Buenaventura, had adopted this delicate method of presenting her with a souvenir.

However, few people object to a little mystery of this sort; so Clem delivered her message, whereat Don Marcos sighed, ' *ab imo pectore*,' applied the palm of his left hand to the white bosom of his shirt, and assured the Señorita that, since she stayed with his cousin, there would be no occasion to divide the seat of his affections; he would leave it entirely in their hands. But Barbara said he had an *otre corazon* in his saddle-bags, which he would offer her before they reached ' El Salado.' So the devotees went their way.

Then the *guëra Inglésa* took tepid chocolate
upstairs to the *guëra Española*, and they became
very fond of each other, though their intercourse
for the last two or three days had not been cordial.

'Dost think that he is killed?' asked the latter,
sipping her chocolate.

'Killed?' reiterated Clem, in amaze.

Nita. Knowest that he is in the mountain?

Clem. Mountain?

Nita. On *my* quest.

Clem. Thy quest?

Nita. Un leoncillo!

'But who is it, dear?' said Clem, stroking her
dishevelled locks.

'Don Carlos. He loves me.' And again Nita
kissed the amber relic piously, and looked enquiringly
at Clem. But the latter was impervious. *She* had
no *liaison* with Don Carlos. On the contrary, she
began to think Juanita a desperate little flirt.

'But, little sister,' she said, reproachfully, 'I
thought Don Marcos loved you.'

'Don Marcos is rich. He loves himself. I love
the poor *Inglés*. I have loved him all my life; that
is, for six long, long months.'

Then Clem, seeing she was in earnest, again stroked
her hair and kissed her forehead, and said softly, 'I
am *so* glad. Dost really love him?'

'With heart and soul.'

'Then listen. He has sixty thousand paistres:

at least, papa has them for him. Be true to your own heart, and let Don Marcos go.'

At this moment the clear ringing voice of Don José came to them—

'*Muchachas! muchachas!*'

'*Tio,*' squeaked Nita, shrilly, '*ven aca, ven aca!*'

The soft firm tread came up the cedar stairs, along the corridor, nearer, nearer; the door flew open: there was a *tableau vivant*!

The Señor Don José at the door, radiant, with a fulvous little puma in his arms; Nita sitting up in bed, shrouded with tawny locks, but stretching out her arms, and shrilling—'*Y Don Carlos? Carlos? Di, tio, di!*—and pretty Clem, in a blue riding habit, and her bright hair wreathed round her head like a diadem.

Don Carlos reposes in the Glade of Oaks. He has killed *una leona, muy grande, muy fiéra.* He is un-hurt.'

'*Ave Maria!*'

As the Señor said, so it was. In one corner of Carlo's bower a hide was stretched, two feet above the ground. There he lay asleep. The glade also was reposing, after profitable labours. The forty acres of barley had yielded eleven hundred bushels, the forty acres of maize two thousand bushels, now stored at the 'Casa Briggs;' for so the small house in the valley had been named.

Now half the glade lay glimmering in the sun, with dusty oat-stubble, amongst which a thousand ground squirrels gleaned in peace; the farther half lay like a broad expanse of gold, traversed by a winding thread of blue enamel, and flecked on either side with black spots of raven, rook, or clamorous crow.

But William Briggs sat by his friend upon a small tripod, such as women sit upon to milk cows. There was a noontide stillness in the air; hard by the ringdove wooed in melancholy tones; and far up from among the cypress groves arose the wailing of the widow-bird.

And William mused incoherently, ' Gold, gold, " thou ever young, fresh-loved, and delicate wooer " of old gentlemen, " thou touch of hearts " paternal! Nita's papa will accept Carlo now. No more cawing crows from morn till eve, and cackling frogs from eve till morn. No more, no more.

' The Casa Briggs is a mere hovel. We must add a wing to it, and touch it up altogether; and I can be god-papa to the bairns as well as the *adóbes*.

' I hope Bernardo has imported those Sonorians, women and all. We want more women and children at this end of the valley. We must fence off a dozen more acres for Cristóbal and Angela, and get some buck-wheat laid down, and give them some more hands.

' If we weren't so far from market, I'd try my hand at making butter. Churning would be famous exercise; and what a fortune a man might make out of these cows, with butter at seventy-five cents a pound!

' This glade has been a triumph. Was it Carlo thought of it, or I ? At any rate, here it is ; and if prices keep up, we shall have cleared fifteen hundred dollars out of it this year, besides our seed-crop, and food for man and beast.

' Then there are the pigs and the vegetables ; " *some pungkins*," as they say in the north.'

When Carlo awoke, and had rubbed his eyes, he saw William thus tilting himself forward on the tripod, and musing. ' Hullo, Will ! ' he observed, ingenuously, ' I've been asleep. What are you doing up here ? '

W. B. Building.

C. Castles in the air ?

W. B. Guess again.

C. A new wing to the Casa Briggs ?

W. B. One to you.

C. I've hit it, then. And you're going to —— eh ?

W. B. [Stroking his beard.] To whom, pray ?

C. Why, to Julia, of course. Don't I know that you're sweet in that quarter ?

W. B. Still there would be many things to consider.

C. What an old deliberator you are ! Haven't you been going to and fro these four months ? And I can see she is interested. Besides which, Miss Clem told me so in confidence. Don't I keep a secret well, eh ?

W. B. You rattle like Marcos. If I *were* ' sweet ' (as you are pleased to call it) on any particular lady, do you think I should ask Miss Clem to feel her pulse? But I have no intention of being 'sweet;' so compose yourself.

C. The sooner you change your intention the better, old boy. Depend upon it, Miss Clem is right; and when you draw off, Julia will think we are all alike, and that the love of a portionless girl has no value for a man.

But William allowed the subject to drop there. 'I'll just light a few sticks,' he said, 'and we'll have a cup of tea.' Whereupon Carlo took a clean towel, a flannel shirt, socks, a comb, and a tooth-brush, out of an old meal-barrel, and retired to his Castalian rivulet.

When he returned, William said, 'I am half angry with you, Carlo. You ought to have taken me last night.'

C. I saw you enjoying yourself at the war-dance, and ——

W. B. You saw me?

C. Yes; I was down there sneaking about on the *pinto.* Shabby trick, wasn't it?

W. B. Why didn't you come with us?

C. I thought I'd have a look at a certain person when she didn't know I was near.

W. B. And you saw?

C. Her standing apart with Julia, weeping.

W. B. Did she see you?

C. Yes; thought I was a ghost. Half thought so myself. Her sadness took me up to the seventh heaven.

W. B. And what brought you down again ?

C. Good old Forina, and put me on this trail.

W. B. The old go-between !

C. Not at all. As my medical adviser, she knew that excitement was good for my nervous system.

W. B. And nearly lost you sixty thousand dollars.

C. How ?

W. B. Starchie got Lord Saltum's letter last night. Old Brownlow left you 12,000*l.*, to be handed over when the trustees should think proper. They 'thought proper' just six weeks ago.

Carlo was sitting on the meal-tub which contained his wardrobe, drinking tea out of a large tin pannikin. He winked over its edge at his friend, and observed, ' Catch an old crow with chaff.'

W. B. There's grain in it, I assure you ; 12,000*l.*

And, looking steadily at William, Carlo saw that he was in earnest. The future loomed before him, as a great glorified mist. Then he felt a fire in his eye-balls, passing down, as it were, to his heart, and again downward till it reached the ground, but left him sear and scathed. It was the anguish of the past.

Putting down the mug, he pressed his hands on his eyelids ; and in that moment of stillness there came again the far-off cry of a widow-bird, bewailing her lot in the forest gloom. ' Hang that bird ! ' he said irreverently.

Then he rose up, and, with trembling fingers, began to caparison the *pinto*. First he put the saddle

M

on too far back, then too far forward; secondly, he twisted the girth, and only fastened it with one strap; and finally he left the horse's black ear outside the frontlet, and the white ear inside; and so would have scurried down the gorge, and galloped to San Pedro, '*ventre à terre.*'

But William made him don the short blue *cha-quéta*, and the *calzonéras* supported at the waist by a crimson sash, as also the elegant deer-skin boots, which were wont to lurk obliviously in the meal-tub; for was it not the feast of Saint Blank? and were not festivities going on at the mansion of Don José?

'Bother the clothes!' fumed poor Carlo. 'Do come and lace up my boots, Will. I've got the palsy.'

But lest the thread of our narrative should fail, we must go back and pick up a stray filament. While Nita was praying to Our Lady of Succour, and two weary horsemen were wending homewards with a laden mule, even while the sun was dissolving the grey mists of night, two *caballéros*, walking in the gardens at San Pedro, met.

One was restoring the tone of his mucous membrane with a puff of fragrant Orinoco; from the nostrils of the other also issued wreaths of incense.

Don José. How goes it, my brother?

Don Mo. Well. And thou?

Don José. I was thinking of thee and thy pretty child.

Don Mo. Ah! Don Marcos is a gallant youth, and loves her well.

Now the Señor might not have shared Don Mariano's enthusiasm on this subject. Indeed, when speaking of the former *Director Suprémo*, to men of his own party, Don José would style him roundly 'Indio' and 'Heretico.' Now, however, he answered courteously.`

'Bah! my brother. Don Marcos is young, gallant, and rich; but will not love thy flower past its bloom. 'Twill wither on the hot plains of San Blas.'

Don Mo. How?

Don José. 'Twill languish for the shade of this valley, and the hand of an English gardener.

Don Mo. How?

Don José. The man hath a lighter hand than that of Don Marcos. The soil is more genial. Let her be.

Don Mo. My only child?

Don José. Will be ever near thee. 'Tis but a ridge of salt [Las Salinas] between. Shalt have other sons, ere yet a grey hair in thy head.

Don Mo. [Sadly.] *No quiero los estrangéros.*

Don José. Dost not love aliens? It is well; but lovest the man that slew the slayer of thy son, that loved thy child, and forbore to speak. Wilt be out-done in favours by an alien?

Don Mo. Thou art persuasive, my brother; stirring the heart to maintain thy cause against itself.`

Don José. Hast a large heart, Mariano; close not the better half.

Then a pause ensued, during which each puffed away solemnly. But Don José rallied: ' Hast wearied of *thy* wife, Mariano ?

Don Mo. [With a start of anger.] Señor ?

Don José. Ah ! brother. Did my father, Don Joaquin, love thee ? Did not thy wife choose thee ?

Don Mo. Ca-rrramba ! Sayest true. Let the girl choose.

Don José. Thy hand, brother.

And they locked hands. Then the Señor Don José, having conquered, proceeded to load his captive with golden chains.

' Knowest, my brother, that this poor *Inglés* inherits property ?'

Don Mo. I knew it not.

Don José. Sixty thousand piastres, or thereabouts.

Don Mo. Es nada ! It is nothing !

And he waved a lordly hand; as one would say, ' I have yielded ; such a trinket hath not bound me.'

Don José. Lord Saltum, the trustee of Don Carlos, is *hidalgo Inglés.*

Don Mo. Es muy caballéro, el povrecito ; no hay dude. [The poor fellow is of gentle birth, no doubt.]

At this satisfactory concession, the gong admonished them, in plaintive tones, that chocolate and tortillas and the ladies awaited them.

CHAPTER XVI.

ELECTRIC SPARKS.

Quien media vez me ofendio,
Entera no ha de contar-la.

SUPPER was eaten at sunset. The *comedor*, or banquet-hall, opened into the piazza, and so on to the lawn, which occupied the quadrangle of the house.

Across this quadrangle Chinese lanterns were suspended on lines, high above the pear-trees and the fountain, giving a festive and grotesque effect to a scene otherwise familiar, and at other times illumined by the moon and stars.

Don Marcos and his cavalcade had returned from San Miguel. They had even attempted to bring the Fray Don Antonio with them; but that functionary declined to leave his few sheep in the wilderness for mere feasting and merry-making.

The party was to break up on the morrow. The Señor Don José would accompany Don Silvestro and his ladies to Monterey, thence to take steamer for San Francisco; the Señor Arianas would return to Los Ojitos; but Don Marcos, with Alberto and his ladies, would go southwards to San Luiz.

Thus it happened that a tinge of sadness mixed with their enjoyment, as the quaint glimmer of the paper lamps mixed with the broad tints of sunset.

Music followed the repast. Again, and for the last time, host and guests seated themselves at will in the dim corridor, or lounged on the glossy boards. The Doña Barbara, as she foretold, had taken possession of the *otre corazon* of Don Marcos; but Carlo stood dreamily by the side of Juanita, who sat on a low settee by the side of Madre. The golden masses of her hair were gathered behind the neck, and fell down her back in two broad plaits, after the manner of the country. Her frock was of simple white muslin, as indeed were those of the other *Señoritas*, and her little white hands were folded peacefully over that terrible engine of warfare, a fan. She looked very meek and penitent altogether, and Don Marcos thought she was hatching some plot for bringing him back to her feet; whereas really her thought ran thus :—

'The Señor Don Carlos, with sixty thousand piastres, is a different person from the poor Carlito of my foolish heart. Now he will return to his native land, will this *caballéro*. *No le faltara otra dama*, another lady will receive him with open arms. He will look back to his wild *Ranchéro* life, and remember me kindly, may be, as a sister, or less. Things are altered now. Methought 'twas a poor *gambusino*, not a rich grandee.'

So Juanita resolved to think no more of her ancient love. Still she was going away to-morrow; he would go to *Inglaterra*, and they should never meet again. If he *had* stayed away unkindly, and given away her little *gage d'amour*, had he not also ridden into the dark wood at night, to gaze upon her alone (did not La Forina tell her so?), and then ridden away to be killed by *una leona muy fiera, escondida*, in the dark, among rocks? and for what?

Under these circumstances she must be calm and courteous, must let him see that she understood the nature of his kindness, and would not trespass on it for the world. She must not seem sad at their parting: for did she not wish to make him less sad formerly, not less happy now? Juanita was a young lady of such inexorable Platonism.

Meanwhile her papa thrummed away on a broad guitar, which three generations had handed down to Don José. He sang a wild romance about a Moorish knight who had killed, so the lady observed by way of compliment,

> —— *mas Cristianos*
> *Que tienes gotas de sangre—*

more Christians than he owned drops of blood.

Carlo heard the paternal strains, but heeded not. The hidalgo's voice far off did seem to moan and rave, and mingled with the fancied moaning of the distant wave. He was conscious of one presence only, hers who sat beside him, with head drooping beneath his elbow, and palms folded in her lap. Light radiated from her; he stood in it, all beyond was dark.

Doña Clem sang that lullaby which we have heard on a previous occasion. Don Guillermo accompanied her on the guitar. It was Clem's own music. Don José was enchanted. When the lady came to that affecting climax—

> While I weep, love, sleep,
> In my fond arms prest,
> Lull'd in my bosom to rest!

—Juanita dropped her fan.

Don Carlos stooped, and gave it to her. Their eyes met. Hers said, ' Is sadness then the heart of joy ?' His said, ' I hear no song. Thou fillest every sense.'

A conversation ensued on the relative merits of the old bards and the lyric poets of the golden age, ' *El siglo de oro*.' It was maintained that the rude simplicity of the *Romancéros* spoke best the heart and sense of a *Ranchéro*, though the classic writers might be more adapted for town-spun fancies.

' But there are gems on the threshold of the golden age,' urged Don José, ' sprinkled there by graceful hands, ere yet the hearts of men grew cold and formal.' Then turning to Juanita, he said, ' Sing thy *cancioncito*, little one.' And he swept the chords, while Juanita simply sang as follows :—

> Are tears of any profit
>   By night or day ?
>   When love hath passed away
> From sight, is aught left of it ?
>   Say, sister, say.

Is love which passeth kinder
   Than grief which stays?
   Thro' lone nights and long days
Sorrow hath nought to bind her,
   Yet sadly stays.

Ah, tell me, sister; truly
   Is sorrow kind?
   Doth she not sadly bind,
That, coming, love may duly
   Due welcome find?

It is not the custom in those regions to thank ladies for singing. Birds warble gladly enough to whom nature has given a voice. Yet Don José said, 'Thanks, little one. Hast the soul of *ruiseñor* * in thy white breast.' And Don Carlos said nothing, but likened her in thought to Saint Cecilia, kneeling 'near gilded organ-pipes,' and to Spenser's fair Saint, at her 'heavenlie virginals.'

His humour was broken in upon by an abrupt change in the proceedings. A small platform raised in the *Estrado* was now occupied by three swarthy musicians, one armed with a violin, another with a wheezy wind instrument yclept *caramillo*, another with the Chinese gong severely muffled for the occasion, and doing duty for a drum. They were reinforced by one or other of the gentlemen, who would take a guitar, and a post of observation near the glass doors, or against a pillar in the balcony.

They struck up a mazurka. Saints defend us!

* The nightingale.

What a strain, in that dim religious light! wax
tapers twinkling within, variegated lamps without;
and the silent summits of San Lorenzo standing
up among the starry heavens. A mazurka! Proh
pudor! To vex a saint at her heavenlie virginals
with such a pastime!

Don Marcos advanced and made obeisance. The
magic light was dispelled. The saint rose, and a
blooming little maid, dropping a curtsey to Don
Carlos, fluttered away like a white moth in the embrace of a dragon-fly; for the integuments of Don
Marcos glistened with bullion, and the long tails of
his purple sash whizzed round and round, as he spun
down the glimmering corridor.

Later on, a feeble attempt was made to introduce
the polka, 'an unblest figure, in which one goes
trotando sin elegancia.' Don Mariano, who was invaluable on the broad guitar, refused to assist in the
performance of such ridiculous music, and called for
the *boléro*; but was induced to compromise in favour
of a 'valse à deux temps.'

Don Marcos still retained the hand of his cousin.
Was he not her kinsman? and if Don Carlos had
wished for her hand, might he not have gone
through the simple ceremony of asking her?

But Clem, having performed a mazurka with the
Señor Don José, came to Carlo, and said, 'Please,
Don Carlos, ask me to dance.' So he asked, she
consented, and away they went. But Carlo gyrated
furiously and silently, for Don Marcos seemed to be

buzzing about his brain like a gad-fly. His partner wished to rest at one extremity of the piazza, so he grimly offered her an arm to lean upon; but she clasped suppliant hands, and looked up into the sad grey eyes with a smile, saying, ' Please talk to me.'

Then he noticed how pretty and bright and kind she was, and his blood upbraided him.

' I beg your pardon, Miss Starchie,' he said, ' do forgive me for being such a Goth; but I was out all night, you know, and have had a terrible shock to-day.'

' A shock ?'

' Yes ; that about the money.'

' A nice shock, was it not ?'

' Well, you don't know how I'm situated.'

' Please tell *me*.'

' You're awfully kind, Miss Clem—beg pardon— Miss Starchie, and I should above all things like such a pretty confidante, but ——'

' " But "—and " above all things "—above Julia now, for instance ?'

Then Carlo fairly blushed, remembering that he had poured out the bitterness of his heart to Julia, in the dark ravine. 'Well, it looks like beating about the bush,' he pleaded, ' doesn't it ?'

' You told that pretty bush, Julia, that the bird had flown, and you won't tell poor me anything ; but I tell you, the bird is there alone, and waits for you to come and rob the nest.'

And as though to deny her consolation, the dragon-fly and the white moth fluttered towards them, spinning round on one pivot, and fluttered away again; and the gad-fly insinuated its probe into Carlo's brain, and perhaps at the same moment into Juanita's; that is, if jealousy may be likened to a gad-fly, and if a fly can be in two places at one and the same time.

After that waltz, Don Alberto proceeded to sing a *seguidilla* with his wife. This performance gave universal satisfaction. Especially to a couple who remained apart, and conversed in an under tone.

Nita. Remember you the squirrel, Don Carlos?

C. Si, señora.

Nita. You gave it me.

C. You paid me with a look.

Nita. I gave it not away.

C. No?

Nita. It died.

C. Poor squirrel, 'twas too happy.

Nita. [Ruefully.] 'Twas happier than I.

For she thought, 'He parries my thrust. Why not confess that he gave her the little cross? I *was* unkind to him, and he gave it her in anger, no doubt.'

But Carlo thought to himself, 'She wants me to understand, though I sent the cross back, and she afterwards gave it away, that she kept and valued my little present till death removed it.'

Again, after a pause, they conversed, she sitting with downcast eyes, he still standing at her side.

C. The night is beautiful.

Nita. [With a sigh.] *Noche serena!*

C. If it could but last!

Nita. How long?

C. For ever.

Nita. You would give the moon and stars away.

C. To you.

Nita. No; to another.

C. What other?

'*Clem*,' she answered, with a little sob; and her breast heaved, and two large tears burst from the fringes of her closed lids, and coursed rapidly down her cheeks.

'Forgive me, madonna,' he said, bending over her, 'I meant not to pain thee. Let her take the moon and stars; but take thou my heart, and the long night will be calm and bright.'

'Art forgiven, *mi hermano*!' she said, smiling celestially. And at that moment Don Marcos came up, smiling too, and claimed his little cousin for another dance.

She went off, thinking to herself, 'He has confessed— "Forgive me," quoth he—Art forgiven, *Carlito mio! mi hermano, no mas. Te quiero, mi hermano, carillo mio!*' and so forth.

But Carlo fell a thinking. 'She doesn't like my being so civil to Miss Clem. How is it? O, I see. Both fair. Thinks I admire the type. Ha, ha! Never found out Clem was pretty at all till just now. And couldn't tell for the life of me whether her eyes are blue, black, or green.' [Those orbs were in fact brown.] 'I'll go and ask Julia to dance.'

But finding that lady engaged, he indulged the querulous humour, and stood scowling angrily at Marcos, whenever that gallant passed his way. ' Suppose after all she only likes me as a brother,' he mused, ' and that Marcos is, in reality, the *objet* ? It looks like it, by Jove! Curse the fellow! with his moustaches and his buttons.'

Now this unreasonable lover having neglected to ask the young lady to dance, yet chose to consider that Don Marcos, by dancing with her, was doing him a personal injury. And revolving this little grievance continually in his mind, he struck off sparks of malevolence, which the other caught in passing.

The exuberant moustache of Don Morcos bristled wrathfully. ' *Ca-ramba !* ' he growled, over Nita's shining head, ' will this lion-hunter shoot me down in the *Puerto del Oso*, and pounce upon my lamb with the golden fleece ? '

Then it occurred to him that Don Carlos had probably discovered the little stratagem which he and his *compadre* Alberto had executed, with the help of that unfortunate token, the amber cross.   His inward monitor said 'twas a foul trick.   Alberto said all was fair in love.

Fair or foul, if Don Carlos had sifted it, he was an enemy ; and if so, one not to be lightly disposed of.

When the dance was ended, this train of thought led Don Marcos through the *Estrado* into the armoury of the Señor Don José.

He rolled a *cigarito*, took the wax candle out of a sconce, carried it round the walls, took down a blade of Tolédo, balanced it, executed a pass or two, swore at it, and restored it to the stand; found a curved scimitar of Damascus, touched the ground lightly with its point, and—

'*No le hace, compañero,*' said the voice of one who entered unobserved; '*es muy Espadéro el Inglescito.*' And the husband of Doña Isabel communicated to his friend a narrative concerning Don Carlos, which he had received from his wife, who heard it from Barbara, who had it from the lips of Clem, who heard it from Annie Briggs, who had it from *on dit* in *Inglaterra* years ago.

We cannot give ear to such vagrant report; but Don Marcos having done so, restored the scimitar and examined the pistols with minute attention. He looked at each one, balanced it, tried the lock, swore at it, and finally pointed to his own heavy revolver, which lay apart in a holster of embossed leather, saying, '*Es mejor. Seis tiros.* Fifteen yards.'

Whereupon the Doña Isabel glided into the room with lissome Barbara, and the moustache of Don Marcos wreathed itself into a smile.

CHAPTER XVII.

THE RETURN OF EL PINTO.

Do los mis amores, do los,
Do los andaré à buscar?

NOW it happened that while Don Marcos was inspecting the arsenal, Don Carlos, leaning submissively against a pillar, was sustaining a rattle of musketry from certain eyes which flashed fitfully over the ramparts of Juanita's fan.

Idioma de amor, some people euphemistically term that exercise. In a short narrative like the present, I cannot find space to gloss over the fact that it is ball-practice at short ranges.

'What *does* it all mean?' enquired Carlo of Reason, helplessly. But that respectable counsellor having been placed *hors de combat*, was unable to reply.

'What a bewildering little siren it is!' mused the helpless one. [The Saint, you see, had shrunk away at the clang of arms.] 'If I were quite sure she wanted to get rid of him, I'd wing that sublime Marcos: 'tis a consummation devoutly to be wished.'

'What *does* she mean by calling me *hermano*, and

peppering a fellow like this?' [In allusion to the musketry, possibly.]

And as far as combatant, under such galling fire, may be said to be conscious of anything, Don Carlos was aware of getting seriously worsted, and was about to surrender at discretion.

Presently the firing ceased, and the fort hoisted a signal. Glad of a respite, Don Carlos (to discard a refractory metaphor) offered his arm to the *Señorita*, and walked away into the silent night. They, too, were silent for a while.

'*Inglaterra*, is it beautiful?' the lady asked, at length.

Carlo thought his island-home would be a dead swamp without this '*dulce enemiga.*'

'Nature is more bountiful here,' he replied, ambiguously.

'Yet one loves the birthplace, the home of childhood,' she persisted.

'Can't say I do,' thought the other, but held his peace.

Nita. [In a low silvery voice.] When shall you return to *Inglaterra*?

C. When thou wilt not suffer me to stay.

'O, *Señor Don Carlos*!' she whispered reproachfully, and clasping his forearm with both her little hands; 'O, *mi hermano*! my brother.'

Footsteps drew near, accompanied by the susurrus of moving muslin. They turned. Don Marcos, with

Doña Barbara, confronted them, with sweet smiles and mellifluous words.

Juanita blushed and quavered, like a rose in the hot south wind; but Carlo smiled grimly, still shooting out sparks of electricity, which sought the buttons of Don Marcos.

'I love not Don Marcos,' he said, as the pair withdrew.

'Nor I,' she murmured, clinging to him timidly.

'Say it again, madonna!'

'I love him not, *mi hermano!*'

And so they returned, and met *tio* Don José walking and talking with *padre* Don Mariano.

Don Marcos was about to dance the *boléro* with Doña Barbara; so Nita entered with her papa and uncle, but Don Carlos turned his back upon the graceful dance, and walked apart among the pear-trees, in the dappled lights and shadows, consuming the solitary weed, and pondering in doubt.

'*Hermano, hermano;* 'tis a pretty word, but I like it not. Yet she loves not Marcos. I will draw the bond closer. I will speak to Madre, to the Señor Don Mariano, this very night, and then — and then——'

But beyond that point the mind of Don Carlos refused to move. There he entered the realms of imagination. On the confines of that enchanted sphere rose the image of Juanita, warm and life-like; the winsome face framed in soft bands of golden hair; the clear blue eye and eloquent lip. Or, when the

eyelid closed, he seemed to feel the music of her
voice, and see the smile between her parted lips.
Around a form divinely moulded the white muslin
draped itself in loving folds. He stretched forth his
arms, and groaned aloud, 'O, Nita! thou must love
me. Not as a brother. 'Twere sin to love a sister
as I love thee.'

This outburst gave vent to suppressed feeling.
His brain began to clear. The image would fade
away. But no: strange to tell, it stood there still, in
the quaint light, leaning against a marble basin into
which the fountain spray was falling like a shower of
diamonds!

'Madonna! Is it thou?' And he took her warm
hand; for indeed it was Juanita herself.

C. Speak!

'*Amigo*,' she answered softly, looking down.

C. Not *hermano*?

Nita. Not if thou wilt not.

C. What did I say, dear?

Nita. I know not. Didst speak in thy own tongue.

C. I love thee, sweet; wilt trust me?

Nita. I trusted thee once.

C. Speakest the truth. 'Twas a new life.

[But the lady pouted her crimson lips.]

C. Pout not. Beg back the token and give it me
again.

'O the shameless one!' she thought; but only
shook her head mournfully.

C. I loved thee.   Was it not well to be silent ?
Look up.   See if I have not suffered.

And looking up, the lady saw indeed traces of a
silent struggle in the expression of his face.

C. But thou wilt not.   'Tis too much to ask.

Hereupon the small hand, which lay in his, closed
round his fingers.   'Not that token,' she said; ''tis
worthless now.'   Then she let go his hand, unfast-
ened a little gold chain, and once more put a fetter
round Carlo's neck, saying, 'Wilt give it away ? '

C. Never.

Nita. Nor lose it ?

C. Never.

Nita. So mayest ever keep my heart.

In a paroxysm of gratitude, the impetuous young
man clasped her round the waist with both arms,
and covered her face with kisses, disregarding her
blushes and frail efforts at escape.

'*O Carlos ! sin-verguenza ! sin-verguenza !*' she murmured ; and as soon as he released her, ran away as
fast as her little red boots would carry her.

And, looking at the end of his fetter, Carlo found
there an amulet, in a case of violet-coloured silk,
which also contained a golden tress.

He was still in the land of enchantment.   An eye
still watched him ; no longer the soft blue orb, but a
black lambent onyx, flashing out of a livid face, and
over the moustache of Apollyon.

The voice of Don Marcos also expressed intense
emotion.   Carlo began to respect him.

Marcos. Art a slayer of men, Don Carlos ?

C. I fight but with enemies, señor.

Marcos. Art my enemy.

C. An thou wilt.

Marcos. Nosotros, cabálleros qui somos, meet face to face, with equal weapons.

C. It is well, Don Marcos ; at break of day.

Marcos. It is well, señor ; *hasta luego.*

The night was far spent before the revellers retired to rest. The Englishmen did not return to Santa Perona: they occupied the first room in that gallery where were the men's sleeping apartments ; the room, in fact, next to that occupied by Julia and Juanita.

After a couple of hours' sleep, Don Guillermo turned restlessly on his bed. 'A grand thing sleep is, in a weary world,' he mused, looking across at his friend. ' That calm sleeper has had a restless time of it. I suppose he has made a land-fall at last. He held on like a man when the wind was foul. Now it's plain sailing ; a harbour as wide as the Golden Gate ; and — *voyons* — William Briggs as harbourmaster. Hullo ! more watchers abroad ! '

Through a small window near William's bed came a sound of ringing chords, sweet and plaintive, then the deep rich baritone of Don Marcos. The tune was monotonous yet impassioned ; the words ran as follows :—

In the sad starlight,
　　Vigil I keep :
By the glad starlight,
　　Sweet my love, sleep!
Chill is the night, love,
　　Sad without thee;
Hast thou in sleep, love,
　　One sigh for me?

Soft are thy lips, love,
　　Sweet is thy breath;
Hard is thy heart, love,
　　Bitter is death :
Yet sweet is bitter,
　　Bitter is sweet;
Soft is death's litter,
　　Laid at thy feet.

In the sad dawning,
　　Vigil I keep,
All the glad morning,
　　Sweet my love, sleep!
Gather thy tresses
　　Of gold to thy breast:
Grey morning presses,
　　I haste to my rest.

Fold thine arms close, love!
　　Sadly I wend,
Sighing for thee, love,
　　Unto my end.
Sighing for thee, love,
　　All the sad night;
Dying for thee, love,
　　In the grey light.

' Dying for thee, love ! ' mused William. ' What is the man maundering about ? '

Then turning to Carlo, and seeing that champion still in a deep sleep, he continued, ' Nothing wrong in that quarter at any rate.'

That there *was* something wrong in that quarter, notwithstanding Carlo's peaceful slumbers, we know. He has challenged Fate to decide between him and an angry rival, this morning. He has no patent for longevity. Let us leave him.

At early dawn the ladies assembled to discuss chocolate, and the journey which awaited them. But amongst them, gathering, Rumour went about whispering strange tidings. Anon they swarmed out in a body, with pale faces and throbbing breasts.

They heard a crash of arms in the valley. They saw the Señor Don José vanishing in the mist on a white horse ; Don Mariano and Don Silvestro standing awe-struck.

Presently there dashed into the midst of them a small horse, which stood riderless, with red nostrils and heaving flanks. It was the barb of Don Marcos.

Juanita's heart thundered in her ears. Horror painted Carlo standing over the corpse of his rival, with close lips and gleaming eyes. She hid a red shameful face in burning hands, and counted the loud pulsations of her heart.

Again the report of arms. Hush ! It came again,

louder and more terrible still. *Madre de Dios!* Could Juanita hear those sounds and live?

A long pause ensued, an age of silent agony and suspense; then the tramp of horses and the ring of spurs came swiftly up the valley.

A figure emerged from the mist: 'twas Alberto. Another: Don Guillermo. A third, coming slowly on the *pinto.*

Juanita's eyes start from their sockets to meet him. She knows the horse: she knows the — *Ah! Jesu Cristo!* who is this?

MARCOS!

Then Carlo has fallen.

A terrible cry rang out of that fluttering crowd; a shriek of woe unutterable; and Juanita fell down, stark and stiff.

There she lay with livid face; eyes open, but cold and hard as stone; lips white, frail body still and lifeless.

'Dead, dead!' they murmured, closing round, and crossing themselves for fear.

Don Marcos stood up in his stirrups and saw this picture.

'*Valga-me Dios!*' he groaned. '*Mi corazon! mi alma!* dead, dead!'

CHAPTER XVIII.

A PASSAGE OF ARMS.

WHEN the serenade of Don Marcos ceased, and
Don Guillermo saw his friend still sleeping in
profound peace, he concluded that the poet was about
to die in metaphor only : but the grey light which
precedes the dawn, and to which the musician had
alluded, literally supervened.

A stealthy tread came along the corridor, the door
opened, Alberto stood in the aperture. 'Quick, friend!'
he said, beckoning to William.

'Wherefore ?' asked the other simply.

Then Alberto drew near, and told William that his
friend had a rendezvous with Don Marcos, under the
great plane-tree, in the river hollow. They were to
meet at dawn. No time was to be lost.

As Alberto withdrew, William looked at his sleeping comrade ; and loving the man, hated the folly of
his act. 'Fighting for a woman's heart! As though
powder and blood could turn the scale one way or the
other! Wrangling at the very edge of doom! 'Tis a
godless act. I won't abet.'

'Carlo !' he called softly.

'Hull-lo!' sighed the other. 'O, Will, I've been

having such a heavenly night, and now we've got to turn out and smell that everlasting saltpetre.'

'I won't go, Carlo.'

'By Jove, then, I'll go alone.' And Carlo jumped out of bed and began dressing. William also dressed silently.

When they were both ready, Carlo turned on his friend: 'Look here, old boy; don't let a shade of anger come between us two, when one may be stepping over "that bourn from which no traveller returns." Marcos forced this quarrel on me, or rather offered it, like a man. I couldn't back out. You know what would have come of it. The man has bad blood in him as well as good.

'Don't think I'm trifling, Will. I'm doing what I believe the least of two evils. This is a fair fight, in an open field; and I at least can stay my hand. I rode to the lodge last night while you were otherwise engaged, and made my arrangements. Cristóbal is, by this, under the sycamore with your long pistols and the French powder. My last testament is here' [tapping his breast pocket], 'writ in plumbago.'

This was the longest speech Carlo had ever made. A tear rose in his eye. He stretched out a hand to William. The other took it, and said, 'I'll come with you; it might have been worse.'

'Thanks, old friend.'

'How about choice of weapons?'

'Each shoot with our own.'

'And distance?'

'Left that for you to settle on the ground. You know it matters little to me.'

Now, in fact, the distance was a matter of the highest importance: for Don Marcos could use his own revolver to perfection at fifteen yards, and with either hand. So William, devoutly wishing that he might put them farther apart, remained silent, not caring to perplex Carlo with these minutiæ.

'You're not savage, are you?' asked William, after a pause.

'Not the least. I like the fellow now I know he's in earnest.'

'Do you think he means mischief?'

'Sure of it.'

As they went down stairs, William said, 'It's too early for milk.'

'Never mind, old boy; I'm all right.'

'A thimbleful of spirits?'

'No: bad for the nerve, and makes the eye fishy. I've tried it.'

But, passing the glass doors of the Estrado, William spied a large decanter of *agua-'rdiente* with a silver cup at hand. 'That looks well for our side,' he thought; 'we will take ours by-and-by.'

They saddled their horses in haste, and mounted. One pointed above the peak of San Lorenzo, where a trembling star grew pale and wan before the coming day. They rode at speed through the low misty level, and found Alberto measuring out the ground.

Don Marcos chatted with Cristóbal indifferently.

Carlo saluted him. Marcos offered a *cigarito* and a light. They smoked amicably, abused the cold fog, voted it a nuisance having to get up so early in the morning, revived light incidents of the past evening, pronounced it to have been a *noche serena*, and regretted the dissolution of such a charming party. Had Don Carlos ever visited the Pueblo de los Angeles? No? There were the vineyards and the orange grove of the Señor Don Mariano, so fair, so fruitful! Don Marcos hoped that Don Carlos would do him the honour to run down the coast in the *Yegua Negra*. He should be cruising on the coast all the autumn. Intended to stock the island of Santa Cruz with sheep, from his estate of San Blas. *Caramba!* How long Alberto was! Time for another cigarito. No? '*Adios, Señor Don Carlos!*'

'*Adios, caballéro!*'

In the meantime William and Alberto tossed for choice of distance. Alberto won, and chose fifteen yards. William gnawed at his beard. There was yet a chance.

W. Fifteen yards is point-blank range with our pistols.

Alberto. It matters not, señor.

W. I must warn you. Don Carlos hits a dollar nine times in ten.

Alberto. Mil demonios! Es verdad?

W. Simple truth, Don Alberto, as you may see presently.

Alberto placed his man nervously, and muttered in his ear, 'Life or death, *compañero*; the saints guard thee.'

Carlo threw aside his *sombréro*, and smiled as William ranged him; but neither spoke a word.

Cristóbal, apart with the horses, shuddered.

Thus they all stood, in the long, damp grass, and round them hung a yellow mist, just smitten by the rising sun.

'*Uno!*' cried Alberto. Up went the two right arms.

'*Dos!*' answered William. Each took aim.

'*Tres!*' A double flash, a horrid din, and a quaking of the mist.

Carlo felt a singing in his ear, as if a musquito had flown into it. It was the whiz of a small bullet, passing within the eighth of an inch.

Marcos felt a dull blow under the right shoulder; then a hot stream of blood pouring down his arm. 'Quick, quick!' he grated out, shifting the pistol, and turning his left shoulder to the front.

William called Alberto aside. 'We are satisfied,' he said. 'Let the matter rest.'

'Don Marcos is wounded: he demands another shot.'

'I warn you,' urged William. But Alberto returned to his principal, and William handed Carlo the other English pistol in silence; the latter still smiling blandly.

' *Uno !* '

' *Dos !* '

' *Tres !* '   A single flash, a feebler din.

Again Carlo felt the singing, and a sharp twinge ; for this time the bullet had passed through his hair and barked his ear.

Then he raised his right arm, and fired the pistol off in the air. The large bullet crashed among the leaves and branches of the plane-tree ; and another horseman emerged from the surrounding mist. It was Don José, spurless, and on a white horse ; but the barb of Don Marcos had fled at the first report.

Don Marcos advanced, holding out his left hand to Carlo, with a gracious smile. ' The *caballéro* has disarmed me,' he said ; I withdraw.' Then languishing, he leant upon Alberto ; for the blood flowed swiftly from his right arm, and he had been up, during the calm cold night, with a tempest raging in his liver, and fire in his brain.

The Señor Don José, with William's assistance, swiftly severed the right sleeve of the *chaqueta*, and drew it off the arm of Don Marcos, while Alberto produced a case of balsam, lint, and plaster, wherewith they stanched the bleeding and bound the wound. The hero was himself again. ' Pardon me, señores,' he said ; ' a little vertigo, nothing more.' The deltoid muscle was severed.

Don Carlos insisted on his mounting the *pinto*. His own horse had fled, and the *pinto* had paces so soft, so undulatory.

The rest moved off the ground; but Don José, seeing a drop of blood fall on Carlo's shoulder, stayed awhile, examined the scratch, and plastered it daintily. So it happened that Don Marcos returned on the *pinto*, and Carlo was numbered among the missing.

CHAPTER XIX.

A WEARY VIGIL.

> We are such stuff
> As dreams are made of: and our narrow life
> Is rounded with a sleep.

FROM this rapid sketch of the passage of arms under the sycamore, and of the return of *el pinto*, it appears that, however chivalrous the practice of duelling may be (as compared with certain other modes of settling a difficulty which prevail in His-pano-American society), it may yet be attended with inconvenient results.

How is it that the ball of Don Marcos grazed the acoustic, instead of entering the optic, organ of Carlo ? that the ball of the latter severed the muscle, instead of shattering the bone of his opponent's arm ? *Quien sabe ?*

Again: harmless and amiable as it was of Don Carlos to throw away his second shot, yet the crash of that report increased the anguish of the innocent, and went before the arrival of Don Marcos on the *pinto*, sounding the alarm for such a heart-shock as well-nigh drove one frail pilgrim across that bourn which her lover had prepared to cross before her.

Juanita was not, indeed, dead, but for many days lay in a state of extreme debility and nervous tension. Despite that venerable quack, La Forina, her father had bled her freely while the fit lasted; and, sooth to say, the skill of the *ranchéro* was mere horse-surgery. He snatched her from the embrace of Death, and nearly laid her in his arms again.

'*Vaya!*' said the crone, in scorn; 'hast slain thy child.'

But the danger passed. The friends went their way : Don José to his Senate, Don Silvestro to his counting-house, Don Marcos to his yacht. Juanita remained with her father, mother, and the Doña Julia.

We will hasten over the intercourse of the invalid and her lover during those latter days. Enough to tell that *his* love strengthened with *her* strength; outgrew and overshadowed all the rest of his being. It was not Platonic, not philosophical, nor sublime. It struck no roots into the sky, but deep into earth, the sweet, sensuous mother of us all. It was a tree whose branches would sway in the storm, whose foliage would rustle in the breeze. It would bud and blossom in the genial spring. In its arms the birds of melody would come and dwell. But it stood, as things of earth must stand, under a gracious heaven, waiting for the fructifying dews and rain and sunshine.

It happened, one day, that while Don Carlos leaned

over the lady, performing some service, a small wooden cross peered from the folds of his shirt.

'Ah!' she exclaimed, fixing her dewy eyes upon it, tenderly.

''Tis a model,' he said, following her look. 'My gross nature will have something to *touch*. See this also.' And drawing it out farther, Juanita saw that it was attached to that very cord which erst held the amber cross.

'Wear it no more,' she said, half in pleasure, half in pain; 'hast an amulet now. Hang the cross up at home, and look at it when thou prayest.'

This was the nearest allusion to the old token which passed between them. Juanita still thought he had given it to another, and that she had forgiven him. He still thought that Alberto had duly returned it.

There was another subject on which he shrank from communicating his thoughts. The Señor Don Mariano, having consented that Don Carlos should become a suitor for his child, still placed a gap of six months between them. 'The *caballéro*,' he thought, 'having property and friends in his land, may return thither, and forget the child. If so, well; if not, well: let him return. I go not. I am in the Pueblo, or on my Rancho: my child is ever with me.'

Nor was Carlo to write to her during the interval. He pleaded with the Don energetically. At last a concession was gained. He might write once. '*Un billete, no mas.* Love dieth not within six moons. Prove it, Señor Don Carlos. If it be love, 'twill live.'

Carlo's heart and reason cried out against this cruelty; but he would not complain. It increased his tenderness and devotion during the brief respite caused by her weakness, and perhaps enhanced the pleasure which he derived from an intercourse so soon to cease.

Don Mariano was impatient to return to Los Ojitos, for he had not long to remain there. His presence was required in his little vineyards at Los Angeles. Juanita was yet too weak to bear the motion of a horse. She travelled in a litter by the side of Madre: the Doña Julia on horseback with the hidalgo. William and Carlo accompanied them through the pass El Salado, and as far as the mission of San Miguel. *Adios! adios!*

On the second evening thereafter, the two Englishmen sat in front of the Casa Briggs.

' *Cuan presto se va el placer*—how quickly pleasure passes !' said the former. The quotation had been a favourite one with them since Don Mariano had punned upon their disaster with it.

C. Yet you had three or four months of it, Will, and I had but a few days.

W. B. You would have finished the triplet,* formerly ; why not now?

---

* *Como despues de acordado*
Da dolor !

C. Well, it does leave one unutterably sad. I think the craving for that sort of pleasure is morbid.

W. B. Adam, 'the grand old gardener,' was provided with a wife.

C. But our case is different. We are two; tried by each other, and not found wanting.

W. B. Still we remain two. A man and wife are one.'

C. Then take a wife, and accomplish your unity. What hinders?

W. B. Shall I tell you, Carlo?

C. Ram your guns, and fire away.

W. B. You saw us waltzing together, on the night before your affair.

C. Rather.

W. B. Those were blessed moments; before the spell was broken. She floated round me, like a zephyr, or the breath of flowers. ' How strong you are!' she whispered; 'you carry me in your arms. Please to let my feet touch, sometimes.' But I could have carried her so through the blissful night.

C. You'd have got terribly giddy, old fellow; but go on.

W. B. 'Do you think me strong?' I asked. ' Surely,' she answered. ' Do you ever, or may you not hereafter, want a strong arm to lean upon?' 'I seek none,' she objected. 'No, but hast found one,' I urged: ' the little Rancho is mine, health and strength and a whole heart are mine; and mine is

thine : wilt be my wife, Julia ? ' We were standing
in the quiet moonlight, away from the foolish lamps
and noise. I saw her tremble for a moment, like a
ripple passing over the surface of smooth water.
Then she smiled in that half-melancholy way of hers,
and said quietly, ' For all this I thank you, *señor*,
but cannot accept it. Let us return.' And we returned hand in arm to the *Estrado*, as if nothing had
happened.

C. Tell me again what she said.

And William told him, in Spanish.

C. ' Can not,' mark you, not ' will not.'

W. B. A will and a way, Carlo.

C. Not always. The girl loves you, I'll be sworn.
But tell me, did you raise the siege ?

W. B. Not precisely. I still hovered about. Indeed, I thought her more beautiful then than ever.

C. [Sententiously,]

> The rose looks fair, but fairer we it deem
> For that sweet odour which doth in it live.

But we confuse metaphors : how went the siege after
that repulse ? [And Carlo imagined that he could
see the great bright eyes of the *Señorita* flashing over
her stockade, and making terrible havoc in William's
forces.]

W. B. Once afterwards, on the night before they
left, we happened to be again alone in the same spot.
' The thought of to-morrow unmans me,' I said ; ' let
me speak again.' But she replied, half sadly, ' Are

you not strong, *señor*? Would you give a weak
woman pain?'

C. And the forlorn hope fell back?

W. B. As you say.

Carlo made no answer, but rammed the fragrant
leaf down into his pipe, and thought, 'Hang it!
when *will* poor old Bill get *rangé*?'

He was growing quite patriarchal.

Presently William spoke again, and this time
somewhat testily for a philosopher: 'Look you,
Carlo; I have done with love this time.' And he
shook the ashes out of a venerable bowl.

C. It remains to be seen whether love has done
with you.

W. B. A burnt child dreads the fire; but when a
man puts his fingers between the bars, the old lesson
gets branded in for life.

C. One consideration seems to have escaped you.

W. B. Tell it, and so let us drop a painful subject.

C. [Fiercely.] Painful, indeed! Did your fingers
go in alone? I tell you they clutched a woman's
hand. She may hide it from you; but 'tis burnt,
Will, and you did it.

And a great groan came out of the tawny beard;
for William was a tender-hearted Stoic, and liked not
the imputation of burning women's pretty fingers.

Let no one malign the race of Achates. It is a
good thing when a man is doing, or about to do, some
wrong, which he dignifies by the name of heroism,
wisdom, or duty, that one at his side should get up

and say, ' Call this what you will, it is wrong : I, the man you love, denounce it.' There is something awful in the voice of a friend. We may shut his mouth henceforth; but he has spoken; and his words go rolling round and round the cavernous heart, awaking echoes in the darkness.

Thus often, in the still night, Carlo's words awoke an echo which might have slumbered in his friend's memory: *'Dolor—da dolor,'* what did Carlo say ? ' She may hide her hand, but 'tis burnt—burnt— *dolor, dolor.'* Then sleep would vanquish memory; and sleeping, he would dream that the season for branding had come round, that he stood at noon-day near a blazing fire, holding the rod, while Carlo dragged a heifer within reach. He planted the hot iron against its flank. Then a jet of smoke and steam ; and when it cleared, Julia was standing there alone, holding out a soft white hand, which the pitiless brand had scarred and seamed. And William would groan in sleep, as when his friend first made the thrust.

If the latter was right in his estimate of Julia's feelings ; if she at Los Ojitos or Los Angeles could have seen the strong man tremble to think he had given her pain ; could have seen how, with the perverseness of a brave heart, he loved her more, now that he had lost her ; the proud girl would have felt that there was, in the wide world, one man who would give his whole heart to her who had nothing to give in return but hers.

But we have no intention of invading Julia's confidence. Before long she may tell her own secret. It will be soon enough, perhaps too soon.

The Señor Don José had left William superintendent of his estate. The charge was not at present an onerous one, for little was undertaken during the drought. But William could ride over sometimes, and confer with Don Pedro, the chief of the Indians; and, in the meantime, half the Pedronians, or more, could migrate to Santa Perona, and assist in building the new house.

'Those rascals,' said the hidalgo, 'grow wicked when they have no good work to do.' But the Englishmen would not accept their labour without recompense, and the Señor would not allow his peóns to take money. 'Give to an Indian money,' he said, ' and he sneaks away to the *pueblo*, or to some other *ranchería*: he drinks, gambles, and breaks the commandments. Keep it from him, give him work enough, and see what a happy creature it is !'

So Don Carlos established an emporium of calico, cotton prints, yellow silk handkerchiefs, knives, scissors, and beads ; of cups, and pots, and pans : all which things were imported by the merchant, Don Bernardo, of San Luiz.

A system of currency was introduced. All labour was paid for by the piece: all payments were made in one or more of the wares. Sunday, which was pay-day, was the merriest day of all, when men, women, and children would swarm round the *casa* during half the forenoon, laughing and joking in a Babel of tongues; gibberish, Spanish, and English, in fair proportions.

For now the Pedronians were engaged on the future family residence of Don Carlos. Some were making *adóbes*, huge bricks of mud, mixed with straw, and baked by the sun : some were making and baking tiles, others sinking a well. And the little grove at the back of the site was vocal all day long ; for the busy housewives were there, and slim maidens, and chattering imps.

Not a tree was felled in that 'home copse' (so they called it); but the two Englishmen, with Cristóbal and one of the recently-imported Sonorians, were up on the mountain-slopes cutting the red cedar, or in among the gorges felling the tough white oak. The widow-bird was startled in her solitudes; squirrels peered wistfully at the intruders, and herds of red-deer flitted through the glades.

In the evenings there were subjects of importance to be discussed. Mr. Starchie and the Señor Don Mariano thought that Don Carlos ought to consult his own interests, and return to England, in order to obtain Lord Saltum's consent to his marriage. Hugo Monteagle, Viscount Saltum, was a bachelor. His funded property was large : the claimants for his favour not more numerous than usual in such cases. His aversion to a subject of Anti-Christ might be assuaged if Don Carlos were to make the attempt in person.

But Carlo would say to his friend, ' What's to be done ?   I don't care about more money.'

W. B. You're not to see the lady for six months.'

C. Still, one is in the same part. of the world. And it's worth something to be with you.

But William declined to consider that second clause. ' They go a hundred leagues south, to Los Angeles, for the autumn,' he said.

C. Pretty name, ' Los Angeles,' isn't it ?

W. B. A meagre consolation, I should say.

C. Then, you know, Marcos is cruising about. He'll make another attempt, depend upon it ; and, hang me if I don't respect the fellow. But I *must* stay within hail, old boy.

W. B. Then you had better write and tell his lordship how strong the bond is, and that you can't and won't break it. Tell him you fought a duel about her, and that her father is only half a heretic, and a lay impropriator. I dare say he'll come round. You might even ask him to come out and be our guest next year, and judge of the lady for himself. He must be tired of that damp moor in Scotland.

So the matter was settled.   Carlo wrote a long letter, but gave up all idea of returning to England in person.

The friends also discussed gravely a new proposal of Don José, that William should accept permanently the office of mayordomo, and reside at San Pedro ; for it had been agreed that Don Carlos should purchase the little *Rancho* of his friend. The result of

their deliberation was, that they should hold together. What mattered it to whom the land belonged?
William should help to stock and cultivate it. William should help to build the new house, still to be
called the '*Casa Briggs*,' and to inhabit it when
built. They would have a common brand. Irons
were ordered with the monogram **MB**, to represent
the firm of Melnot and Briggs.

The site of the new house also had been eagerly
discussed. Carlo wished to leave the *casa* as a
southern boundary lodge, and to choose a site nearer
the *hacienda* of San Pedro. William opposed this:
it would be dividing their strength too much.
Either Cristóbal's site he would have, or the old
one.

C. I tell you I want a garden; and we haven't
water enough up here.

W. B. Did you ever notice the fountain in the
court at San Pedro?

C. Didn't I tell you it was playing about her like
a shower of diamonds when I—you know?

W. B. So you did. A very pretty simile. Where
did you get it?

Carlo made an attempt to claim that illustration
as an original: but William waived the subject, and
went on: 'Well, I won't press you. We'll have a
fountain, too. Have you ever thought about these
lagoons in the sand-hills?'

'How the fellow does wander!' thought his
friend.

W. B. Splendid sheet of water the Agua Muerte is! Supplied in the same way. These Sierras are the walls of a great underground watercourse; and wherever nature has bored, or man shall bore, a hole down to it, up the water comes.

C. You'd have saved Babylon.

W. B. I would keep this site, and even the old hovel itself, if I might.

C. Then not a patch of its sacred mud shall be touched, old boy; here we'll live and die.

W. B. No, thank you. No. Let us build on the old site, as we pile fresh experience on the ground of old memories.

C. And nettles that we thought dead crop out among the roses.

W. B. Ay, or roses among the nettles.

C. Laudator temporis acti.

William smiled at the rebuff. 'Carlo is right,' he thought. 'The past stings like an ungracious nettle. The present bears its thorns and roses on one stem.'

Sometimes of an evening William would ride over to the *hacienda*, and fraternize with Don Pedro, the Indian chief, or visit La Forina and her maiden staff at the great house. At others he would withdraw to the copse at the back of the *casa*, where the Pedronian colony was encamped; and in that curious society he would be merry, profound, or sentimental, as the humour seized him.

On these occasions Carlo would work at his plan

for the house, would muse, or write his letters. Amongst others he wrote his one letter to a certain young lady; and I have since been informed that the *donzella* laughed and cried over the simple performance. But her emotion may be in part attributed to circumstances which had taken place on the little *Rancho* : and in order to present these vividly to the reader, I must sketch some leading features of the scene and season.

The great *Hacienda* of San Pedro, with the smaller estate of Santa Perona, form together a tract twelve leagues in length, by an average breadth of seven leagues. It may be described as a plateau lying between two sierras, that of the Monte Diablo on the east, and of Las Salinas on the west.

The foot hills and slopes of the Sierra del Monte Diablo are richly wooded near the bases with white oak; higher up, with fir, cypress, and cedar. Below the ridge lies the long valley of the San Lorenzo, clothed during eight months of the year with grass and clover, which fail during the autumnal drought. But the western part of the plateau is broken into undulating masses, interspersed with large lagoons.

The latter tract is not entirely barren. In the spring thousands of acres are covered with luxuriant wild oats; but where the soil is rocky, or sand-hills [*medanos*] rise and fall, the vegetation is confined to patches of cactus, mescal, and a stunted juniper, or here and there a clump of shrivelled holm-oaks.

We are now far advanced in the long drought,

which lasts from May till October. The aspect of the country has passed from green to yellow, from yellow to a greyish brown ; and where your horse's feet used to dash the dew from long grass, or leave a track through green pastures of wild oats, a cloud of dust now marks your passage. The dry soil cracks and gapes. The coyote leaps out of crevices. Ground squirrels scurry into innumerable little holes, at which a small grey owl stands sentry.

Only down the valley a long line of poplars and willows mark the course of the river, which has now dwindled to a narrow stream, winding along the central channel.

From the Casa Briggs to San Pedro the trail runs almost in a straight line for two leagues, passing the lodge and gardens of Cristóbal, but is lost sight of beyond the boundary, in a forest of oak, which occurs in this part of the valley, forming a natural division between the pastures of San Pedro and Santa Perona.

But green grasses are now only to be seen in hollows where the soil is rich and loamy. There, under willow or poplar, ringdoves congregate, and make perpetual music ; but the cattle, avoiding the rank unwholesome grass, shun these spots. The great steppes become a wilderness. Wild oats and grass seeds, which strew the ground, are good fodder for mules and horses ; but the cattle become lean and wild. Cows conceal their calves in the scrub growth of the sand-hills, and stray into the open country or the mountain spurs in search of pasture : numbers of

them falling victims to the bear, the puma, and the
wolf, which grow fiercer as the season advances, and
come boldly among the haunts of men.

Feræ naturæ abounded on all sides. Two colts
were cárried off from the lands of San Pedro. Calves
were devoured among the mescal and juniper bushes,
where they had been concealed. A favourite cow
was killed within a hundred yards of the casa. The·
carcase was poisoned freely with strychnine ; and the
two friends lay in ambush all night, with bullets in
their guns and fury in their hearts, in vain. At
daybreak the coyotes rushed upon the prey, and
devoured it, five of them falling dead on the spot.

A few days afterwards, while now September was
drawing to a close, a body of Pedronians, mounted
on the swift steeds of the *hacienda*, accompanied by
Don Guillermo and Cristóbal, rode westward to keep
the Vigil and Feast of San Miguel, at the mission.
The rest of the Pedronians returned to their *ranchería*;
but Don Carlos remained at home, with a couple of
his own men.

Day yielded to night. Manuel and Francisco
slumbered in the porch. The dogs lay round the
fire. Over it Carlos stood moodily, brewing tea.
' Confound the bears ! ' he thought ; ' to kill Josefita,
a pretty tame cow, that one had got quite fond of ;
and then, after putting one to the expense of all that
" nux," not to come back again ! The skulking
brutes ! '

And he began to plot against his own word. ' Fool

that I was to promise not to hunt one again! Now
I followed that track right across the *medanos*, and
I'm certain they go to water at the Agua Muerte.
If I *should* happen to be in the way when they come
down, why a scrimmage might ensue. Do I provoke
it? No. A chap shoots wild fowl on his own
waters: no one can object to such a pastime.

'But I don't generally shoot teal with a rifle. It
won't do. Yet the long duck gun would throw a
bullet hard, at close quarters. I'll sew one or two
up in leather, and slip them into my pocket. They
can't do any harm there.

'Confound the bears!' he continued, having scalded
his throat with some hot tea. 'Seven calves done for.
Two in Salt Valley, one in Sandy Gulch, one in those
dead-alive holm-oaks; *that's six*! and three in the
scrub—by Pan, *that's ten*! Why can't those black
harpies * show, before they get killed? One always
knows where to find the skin and bones. And all to
come out of our lot: every head, by Jupiter! not
one shall the Arianas lose.

'Hullo! How I do growl! Hide thy sweet ears,
Juanita. "*Descanso de mi sentido!*" I'll be trans-
formed into a ringdove. Butter shan't melt in my
mouth.

'But what will the Don think of us? Two fillies
gone already; and his peöns working here all the
time. I don't believe Will rides round the place at

* Vultures.

all, or that any of them have seen the horses or
mares for a week, till to-day. I *will* go after another
puma, by Jove! I'll ride to San Miguel, and get
absolution for a lie. Wonder whether the Padre will
absolve a heretic!'

From which reflections it would appear that the
young man had made a rash promise which he regretted. But his meditations were suddenly checked.
A dismal howl burst from the jaws of three lean
mongrels, which were, or feigned to be, asleep at his
feet. The pipe dropped from his mouth. The dogs'
tails oscillated. Manuel and Francisco groaned.
The curs sprang to their feet, squinted at each other,
took courage, and dashed off towards a dark object
which loomed in the *adóbe* pit.

Rushing into the house for a pistol, Carlo hurried
after, and found the dogs yelping at a huge bear,
which sat upright on its buttocks, grinning horribly.
He kicked the dogs aside, and fired right into its
breast. The bear gave a playful snort, whisked
round, and shambled away in an uncouth gallop.

But Carlo's rifle was loaded, and his blood was up,
probably where his brains ought to have been: so he
took a bridle to the shed, mounted the 'divinest
pinto,' and gave chase. He rode the startled horse
barebacked, and belaboured its sides with his spurless heels. Soon they overtook the dogs. Bruin
was making over the sand-hills, but his weight gave
the pursuers an advantage in the light soil. Presently horse and dogs came to a sudden check, for

the bear had turned to bay, and they were nearly on to him.

When the *pinto* saw this horrible enemy [Ursus candescens] sitting erect, with shaggy locks and gleaming tusks, it reared bolt upright, and fell backwards; but Carlo glided off while the horse was poised in air; and looking, he saw the bear, as he afterwards told William, 'bowling away at the rate of sixty miles an hour, like a small simoom taking a starlight trip.'

'Parbleu!' exclaimed the dismounted horseman. The *pinto* had scampered off in one direction, the bear and dogs in another; he was left alone in a dim desert of dust. Above, the stars shone brightly, indeed; but a rifle was useless, for there was no moon.

So he tramped homewards, musing: 'What could have scared the old bundle of oakum? I couldn't have hit him without putting the muzzle into his mouth. He made light of the pistol-shot, too. *Asi me estoy*: "He who fights and runs away, lives to fight another day."'

Carlo's slumbers that night were not presided over by the winsome face. In his sleep, a dark shadow seemed to flit between him and the stars. Once, he thought, it stooped over him, and grasped at his heart. He shuddered, yet did not wake, but turned over, and slept on.

So the night wore away. This was the Vigil of Saint Michael.

CHAPTER XX.

SAINT MICHAEL TO THE RESCUE.

Alas! that neither tears nor vows
Can certify possession.

'THE Feast of Saint Michael—eh?' murmured Carlo, as he awoke, a little after daybreak. 'Is it *el soldado*, or the angel? Angel, I believe; and that reminds me of Angela. I'll go and have breakfast with her. She's always glad to see a fellow. And isn't the little woman fond of HER? That's all.

'Talk about pumpkins and water-melons,' he continued, 'if it weren't for what they give to the cows, down there, we should have a murrain amongst them; and as to tomatos, there's enough to cure a fever with looking at them. By-and-by we shall have pears, and almonds, and oranges.

'*Mira usted*, Señor Don Carlos!' he went on, apostrophising himself facetiously, 'Orange blossoms!'

And having made his toilette, he took a long single-barrelled gun, and rode off for the boundary, well aware that those pious rogues, Manuel and

P 2

Francisco, would do no work on the high day of the patron saint.

The colony at the boundary of the two estates had grown; two families having been imported from Sonora by Don Bernardo. They had run up a *ramada* * by the side of the log-house, and the three families lived in a cluster; for the new-comers were Angela's countrymen and women, and Cristóbal, a born Californian, was *buen compañero* with everybody.

They worked, as well as lived, together. The small boys and girls carried melons and pumpkins from the garden, and stowed them in cunning layers, with maize-straw between each. The women cut open, and dried in the sun, thousands of bright tomatos. Men and lads worked at the sunk fence, which was to enclose a dozen acres more, to be sown with wheat in the early spring.

But to-day, no works, except of necessity, were done. Outside the enclosure, pigs and cows waged war for pumpkins which the little boys were rolling across the chasm on grooved planks. Carlo rode through the combatants, and installed himself in the porch. 'I am weary of melons, Angela,' he said; '*Hay tanta abondancia.* Give me a *tortilla* and the *miel de Saguarro*: and give me a gourd of sweet milk; for the bears have killed Josefita, and the other cows are dry.'

* Bower.

So Angela produced her 'honey,' which was indeed the syrup of a great Sonorian cactus, and *tortillas*, and fresh milk; hovering round him like a brown guardian angel, loving him, and happy in his service.

He talked, while he ate, about her *hombre*, and about her boy, and her new friends from her 'beautiful country' (the hypocrite had never seen it); then he wished them all Holy Day. He was going across the *médanos* to the Agua Muerte, to shoot duck. Would pretty Angela like some ducks for supper, or for Cristóbal's breakfast? Thomasito could go with him and bring back the horse. He would walk back at night. Only two little leagues, and the stars were bright. Had not the mayordomo two *cuchillos*?

Yes; the Señor Don José had given him a grand one with a silver handle. Here was the ancient one with the long keen blade. Should not Diego go and stay with the Señor? Here Angela looked gravely at the brass carbine. 'Diego can shoot.' 'No, no;' Don Carlos wished to be alone. There was no danger. He would dream away the day. He had been up half the night. ''*Sta luégo, Angela!*'

The boy jumped on to the horse's loins. Carlo carried the long gun across the saddle-bow, and they went over the sand-hills to the great lagoon. Then the child slipped into the saddle and galloped home.

In the centre of the lake appears a long island of bulrushes, with a dense wall of stiff green sword-flags.   Round this lie the still waters fringed with a narrow border of rank vegetation.

On the hither bank three tall poplars have grown up in the most favourable spot ; and near these a willow bends over its reflex in the water.

On the farther side the shore rises abruptly, in rocky ledges, flecked with patches of juniper, and throwing out in bold relief a giant sycamore,* with its silver bark and lush-green leaves.

Above this oasis glows the autumn sun, and all around it rolls a barren waste of sand.

Carlo sought the shade of the sycamore, and loaded his gun.

At his first disturbance a couple of wild geese rose on swift noiseless wings, and vanished in the glare of sunlight.   Now a perfect stillness prevailed.   All the irritation, the foolish anger, of last night had worn itself out.   'Who am I, to murmur,' he thought ; 'bedesman of such a bountiful Giver ? '   The idyll of this morning, and Angela's gentle voice, had soothed him.

He gazed on the tranquil water, heard the call of moor-fowl, saw the drakes leading out files of duck from the stiff green wall of flags, saw the little argosies sailing within easy range, but cared not to disturb them.   'After all,' he mused, 'one must lose a calf or two, and now and then a colt, may be, in the dry season.   The bears must live ; so must the lions,

* Platanus occidentalis.

as they call them. I ought not to have given that
promise; but she will absolve me now, seeing that I
can't keep it. And I don't wonder at her being
timid. If one failed to dodge the spring of a puma,
one's brain-pan would be smashed. It's touch and
go, literally. But bears are another thing.'

The little adventure of last night lowered the great
race of 'grizzlies' in Carlo's estimation; perhaps
prematurely. But he mused on: 'I wonder when I
shall hear from her.

'Let us see—they'll leave my letter at San Miguel.
There are plenty of people passing up and down now,
on the other side of Las Salinas. It will get to San
Luiz by the end of the month, or before, and will
catch the down steamer on the first, so that she will
have it on the fourth.'

*   *   *   *   *

'Can't think what she saw to like in me. Alberto
is not a good fellow; yet he's good-tempered, and
sings like—who was it? Orpheus, eh? And there's
El Mejicano (the Señor Don Marcos), a perfect
rogue of canzonets. Ha, ha!'

And Carlo smiled grimly, thinking of the duel.

*   *   *   *   *

'So that modern Sphinx has refused Will! It
beats me. Yet she loves him, I'll be sworn. I could
see her great black eyes watching him about when
he moved, and her forced calm when he came near
or spoke to her; as if she was afraid of betraying a
secret! Miss Clem told me the same thing too.

That young lady knows a thing or two. Hullo! There's a chance.'

Whether a shoal of small fish, or a few myriads of persecuted tadpoles, had taken refuge in that part of the lake, I am unable to say; but a concourse of various tribes and families of ducks was assembled under a bough of the sycamore; some apparently asleep, others standing on their heads in the water, others disappearing altogether, and popping up again in unexpected places. Suddenly a stick fell amongst them. One of the sentry birds gave warning, and the whole concourse retreated swiftly, in good order, skimming along the surface of the water, and disappearing amongst the flags.

But the long gun commanded the line of retreat. A charge of shot rattled along it, and five dead birds floated on the water, with drooping heads.

Carlo blew down the muzzle of his gun, and as he loaded again, one might have heard him talking to himself: 'One wife's all very well, you know: but polygamy on such a large scale; can't encourage it.'

Then the philosopher produced four little maize-puddings, which Angela had pressed upon him in the morning. Each one was neatly folded in a leaf of maize, and tied round the middle with the fibre of another leaf. They had been boiled perhaps a month before, in these pretty wrappings, and now came out, clean and cool, like jelly from a mould.

He regarded them affectionately. 'Ah,' he thought, ' famous little puddings they are too. Remind me of

Los Ojitos. Didn't we have them there? Of course we did. Don't I remember as if it was to-morrow, I mean yesterday, how *she* put them on my plate, with a large wooden spoon, and just peeped at me with those celestial eyes? Parbleu! it makes one giddy to think of her in this scorching sun.'

For although he had only fired one shot, Carlo had been there a long time, musing and soliloquising. The sun was gilding the tips of the tall poplars on the opposite shore; and only one branch of the sycamore, with its thin broad leaves, gave him shelter.

'And now I come to think of it, these puddings were wrapt in little bits of calico at Los Ojitos.' But here Carlo shut his teeth firmly, and fixed his eyes on a clump of *chaparral* a few yards above, and rather on his right. A minute or two elapsed, but there was neither sound nor motion. 'Pshaw,' he muttered, 'I'm nervous after my vigil; and serve me right too, for a *parcus de*——'*

But again an ominous sound from the *chaparral* arrested his attention. The angry grunt of a grizzly bear—not a snort: Carlo knew the difference well. He took out a bullet already wrapped in leather, and rammed it down on the top of the shot. 'Hang it!' he thought, 'how my hand shakes!' A fragment of loose rock rolled out of the bushes, bounded down the slope, and plunged into the deep water.

It suggested an idea to Carlo. Keeping his eye

* The speaker was about to call himself a 'Parcus deorum cultor.'

fixed on the dangerous spot, he slipped off boots and jacket.   Again all was still.

'Oh ! you won't come on, won't you ?' he thought, stepping out of his *calzonéras*.   Then a tremendous roar shook the very leaves on the sycamore ; and the enemy advanced, with his head down, but stopped within twenty yards of Carlo, tearing up the ground with his fore feet.

The other was kneeling with his gun rested on a rock.   'Bluster away as much as you like,' he cried aloud, in a clear bantering tone ; ' but don't come too near, or, by Ap——'

But the bear advanced, slowly and surely, snuffing the ground as he came.   Carlo pressed the trigger ; the heavy-shotted gun recoiled on him with a loud crash, and springing down the bank, he leaped headlong into the lake.

Striking out vigorously for the opposite shore, he swam for some distance under water, to mislead the enemy.   But no sooner did he rise to the surface than a great sough was heard behind, then a belabouring of the water, which sounded like the paddle-wheels of a large steamer.

He swam swiftly and well, but as the water trickled out of his ears he heard more plainly ; and the awful sounds seemed to gain upon him every moment.

In passing the flags his bare knees glided for some moments over a slimy substance, after which he was again in deep water.   Now the sounds in the rear became stationary and peculiar, like an escape of steam under water. Carlo guessed that his unwieldy foe was in the mire, but swam on steadily, without turning.

Clambering out in shadow of the poplars, he looked back, and saw the bear distanced, by having been obliged to tack, but now plunging through the deep water, towards him, with terrible eagerness. He embraced a poplar, and climbing the tall stem, seated himself, with sore skin and aching bones, on the lowest branch.

Now the bear was heaving his huge body out at Carlo's landing-place; but the bank gave way with him, and he fell backwards. Again, with a furious grunt, the fore paws were planted; up rose the broad back, but again the rotten bank yielded, and back the monster fell, with a splash which sent the spray up to Carlo on his bough.

'What a clumsy it is!' he muttered, and watched the other's movements curiously.

But now the bear chose firmer ground, and emerged. His shaggy locks clung to him dripping with water; but Carlo noticed that blood was flowing from his mouth and staining the ground. He came roaring to the foot of the tree, looking up with an expression of ghastly rage, and the long grizzled beard dripping with gore.

'What *can* the old brute want?' But it soon became evident what he wanted, and then Carlo's blood began to curdle; for the slender tree quivered and shook as the bear, with terrible roars, worked round it, digging a deep trench with demoniac strength, digging fiercely with those huge fore feet, hurling the loose soil and broken roots behind him.

Carlo's gaze was riveted for a while on this mighty delver. 'My hour is come,' he thought; 'I can't fight, naked, and without a knife.' [Fearfully the tree swayed to and fro.] 'Stay : one more chance. If it *should* fall in the water. I'm so good at swimming.' And again he began to climb the shaking tree, keeping his body on the shady side, and jerking backwards each time it swuug that way.

A bear, with its lower jaw broken, and its tongue riddled with duck-shot, is in no humour to temporise. This one toils away with fearful rage, seeing nothing but a prospect of swift vengeance, uttering a continuous roar.

But a coil tightens round its neck; the roar is subdued to a stifled groan ; still it clutches the tough roots, constant to its thought of vengeance. Now it is choking. The small grey eyes start from their sockets, out hangs the gory tongue ; a man approaches within two paces ; a large bullet crashes through its skull; and it lies down dead, still grasping the foundation of Carlo's refuge. For William and Cristóbal, returning early after mass, had heard the ominous sound, and turned their horses towards the Agua Muerte.

So it took three men and two swift horses to kill that bear; but the former congratulated each other as if they had performed a feat of arms. After skin-

ning the monster, Cristóbal took the head on his
saddle-bow, and went for a horse for Don Carlos, and
for a mule to bring home the hide. The other two
went over to the sycamore; William by land, leading
his tired and frightened horse; Carlo by water, 'To
wash the blood off my legs; that bark scratches, I
can tell you.'

He collected the birds on his return, and wrung
out his dripping shirt on the bank; but while he
dressed, William kept sending up a little purple
column between himself and the crests of Las Salinas,
which were fringed with fire by the setting sun.
Then Carlo took the pipe out of his mouth, saying,

'Let's have a whiff, Bill. I'm thinking where I
should have been if you fellows hadn't turned up
just when you did.'

W. B. You were like to have another squeeze for it.

C. A squeeze and a squeak this time. There the
tale would have ended.

W. B. What did you think about, up there?

C. You see I'm getting practical. At first I
thought it was all up. Then I thought the tree
leaned a little towards the lake, and that if it fell
that way I'd keep swimming round the island in
shallow water.

W. B. But didn't you think about anything else?

C. No: I was too busy skimming up the tree and
jerking at it when it rocked my way. I didn't see
either of you till I heard the bark of that glorious
pistol. Then it all flashed upon me, and I thought—

[A pause. Carlo is gazing at Hesper, in a sea of gold.]

W. B. Yes : you thought ?

C. That was heaven over there, and you were two angels sent to deliver me.

W. B. Perhaps we were.

It is pleasing to reflect that the attributes with which Carlo endowed his friend and mayordomo did not impair their appetites. Angela roasted the ducks and stewed the beans, on which rescuers and rescued alike feasted. Don Guillermo told how Cristóbal took the lead on *el negro*, and lassoed the bear ; but Cristóbal related how the Señor dismounted with a single pistol, and shot the furious beast through the head, as coolly as if it had been a steer, or a great 'bundle of oakum,' as Don Carlos facetiously called it.

The latter was now in a joyous mood, and laughed at his own discomfiture. He told them after what manner he kept the vigil, and brought tears of laughter to the eyes of Angela : but Don Guillermo was very grave.

CHAPTER XXI.

LOST AND SOUGHT.

Torments me still the fear that love
Died in its last expression.

THE two Englishmen rode home slowly, in the quiet night, talking.

W. B. One thing perplexes me, Carlo.

C. Let's have it.

W. B. You don't seem to have thought of *her*, once.

C. [Meditatively.]   It *is* queer.

W. B. Can't you account for it?

C. I was in too great a funk, I suppose.

W. B. You haven't lost the chain she gave you?

Carlo tore his shirt open, clutched about his breast with tremulous fingers, felt the bitterness of vexation rise in his throat, the shadow of coming evil steal over his heart.

C. I'm done for.   *The Amulet!*

W. B. What amulet?

C. O!   Don't you know?   Instead of the cross,

she gave me a large opal amulet. It had been in Madre's family for ages.

W. B. And is it gone ?

C. Gone.

W. B. When did you see it last ?

C. Last night, or rather this morning, at three o'clock. I had it in my hand : that's how I got to sleep after my scrimmage with the bear.

W. B. And the chain was round your neck ?

C. Positively, and the end of it between my fingers. You know *she* used to wear it.

W. B. Who was with you ?

C. Only Manuel and Francisco.

W. B. None of the Pedronians ?

C. Not one.

W. B. And when you sponged this morning ?

C. I—I can't remember having it on.

W. B. Yet it might have been all right. A man seldom remembers taking his boots off, and putting them on again.

C. It's upset me, awfully, Will. I'm quite sick.

W. B. Angela puts too much fat with the *frijoles.* [But seeing the haggard look on his friend's face, William added] I never failed you yet, Carlo, did I ?

C. Never.

W. B. Then trust me now. We will either get the opal back, or the loss shall not affect you.

C. [Laying hold of William's bridle-arm.] You know what it is I fear ?

W. B. I know it. Will you trust me ?

C. Yes.

As they were nearing home, William said, 'Don't seem to suspect anything when we get home. I'll do my best.' But the loss had fallen upon Carlo like a heavy blow : it sickened and stupefied him.

The two Indians awaited them, sitting over the camp-fire. They made tea, and produced a little milk which they had reserved.

William told the story of the man-hunt, the death of the grizzled hunter, and lauded the cast of Cristóbal.

Ah! Los Ojitos was the spot for *vaquéros.* Sonora might be well for gardeners, but give William California for herdsmen. So he drew them on.

And women! Industrious, cheerful, skilful, were the women of the country, the daughters of the land. And for savoury dishes [Here William made as though he were stirring a savoury mess over the camp-fire]—*preciosas son las mugeres !*—the dear creatures are invaluable !

There was no restraint, no suspicion; the *vaquéros* glowed with animation. The Señor was right: for *tomatas,* for *pinole con léche,* for *frijoles,* for beef stewed with the *chili colorado,* there were no women like the daughters of the land.

Carlo drank his smoky tea with a wry face.

'The Señor Don Carlos and I are agreed,' continued William: 'on the day of his marriage I give a hundred dollars to Manuel, a hundred to Francisco;

Q

Don Carlos gives a hundred to the *donzella* of
Manuel, and a hundred to the other damsel. Is it
not well ? '

Carlo nodded assent grimly. But the *vaquéros*
were overwhelmed. ' *Dos cientos pésos!*   What words
were these !'

Had not the mayordomo received two hundred ?
Had not Manuel and Francisco forgotten that they
were *vaquéros* ; had they not become carpenters,
builders, what not ?   Had they not guarded Don
Carlos in his sleep ?

But the keen eye of Don Guillermo only encoun-
tered sheepish looks. The men remembered how
that amiable Señor had rated them last night on his
return from a bootless pursuit. *Lastima !* Why
had they not given chase ?

Well, they must each choose a wife, a young
Pedronian with flowing hair, a *muchacha* from San
Miguel, a *donzella* from Los Ojitos. Two hundred
dollars ! 'Twas a pretty sum. Five milch cows
were worth no more.

But Carlo returned to his own pallet in the dim
chamber, and William found him leaning out of the
little window, murdering the tune to which Marcos
had serenaded his love on that dewy morning at San
Pedro. After a time he lay down to sleep, but this
dialogue would repeat itself in the stillness :

' Wilt give it away ?'

' Never.'

' Nor ever lose it ?'

' Never.'

' So mayest ever keep my heart.'

At length he fell into a feverish troubled sleep, and again he dreamt that a shadow came between him and the stars; and this time he roused himself and looked, but only William was near him, sleeping on the other pallet.

In the morning he awoke with hot temples and throbbing pulse. ' Shall we search the place ? ' he said.

W. B. Only where you may have laid it down. I don't suspect them.

C. Then I must have lost it in that poplar. My thighs are awfully sore. Let us go and search.

W. B. We will go after breakfast. Seem at your ease now. We shall get it back.

As they rode away, the two Indians resumed their functions at the saw-pit; one standing below, blinded with the dust, the other straddling over him, with menacing gestures, sawing beams of the great Taxodium, beams and rafters for the Casa Briggs.

The Englishmen rode towards Agua Muerte, by the boundary. There William drew Angela aside for a moment. Then he exchanged a few words with Thomasito, bestowing praise on the little swine-herd. The services of Cristóbal were next enlisted. They were going to see if the vultures had any tales to tell. They might meet with bear or lion. *Quien sabe ?* Three men were better than two.

The sunk fence would progress without the mayordomo? O yes: his *compadres* were zealous to enclose the land while the soil was light and dry. So off they started.

And while the rest heard nothing but the jingling of their bridle-reins and spurs, William was telling Cristóbal of the lost amulet. The mayordomo had heard of the talisman before. They would search under the sycamore, where Don Carlos threw down his clothes; at the bottom of the lake, where Don Carlos took the precipitous leap into it; the spot where he landed; the poplar; the ground all round it; and would find the amulet, by our Lady's help. They would begin the search without Don Guillermo, who was pressing on to San Pedro, but would join them after noon.

So William wound through the *medanos*, seeking San Pedro by another trail; but these two arrived at the great lagoon. With work before him, Carlo came to life.

First they searched under the sycamore, and for some distance round, even to the green border of the lake. Cristóbal had great hope here. In taking off the shot-belt, the Señor's hand might have caught in the chain, and passed it over his head too. Intent on the danger, he would not have missed it.

C. But it is not here, friend, see! Do we not seek?

Cris. But a chain may be dragged. A foot may have caught in it.

So they sought diligently, marking out the rugged

hill-side in strips, twenty-two yards in length, with their lassos, examining it strip by strip, to the water's edge. Not a glimmer of gold, in shade or sunlight, could they see.

Oris. And the rays of light would flash on the amulet.

O. No; it is in a little bag of faded silk, but the chain is bright.

Again Carlo took the headlong plunge; feeling before him with his hands, striking upwards with his feet. The hole was deep, and one long sinewy root of the sycamore formed a bar across it. This the diver grasped, and felt it all down, beginning in the hollow bank, not leaving it with his hands till he had traced it many inches below the slimy bottom. Then he rose cautiously to the surface, anxious lest he should disturb the mud.

Cristóbal's cheerful face met him on the bank; the black eyes flashing expectation, and white teeth gleaming through the jet moustache. It gave Carlo heart.

Oris. Lastima that a *vaquéro* cannot swim! Would that I could dive like a Coco-maricopa!

Carlo. [Panting for breath.] If the who-whole nation of Co-coco-pa were here, it co-could avail nothing. I wu-will find the ch-charm.

Oris. [Stooping over the amphibious lover.] 'Tis a blessed charm. My wife has told me of it. When evil comes to the good house, 'tis like the *lapis lazuli*: when good is at hand, it burns like a heart of fire.

Down glided the supple Carlo into the profound recess behind the root. The water hummed in his ears. His hands moved softly through the slime. Still too soon the water was discoloured. His eyes grew dim; closed; he groped in utter darkness. The flood roared in his ears; the skin tightened round his chest; in ten seconds it would burst.

Cristóbal wondered upon the brink. Clouds of light mud rose up and rolled about in the bright water. A long, long suspense. The mayordomo could hear the loud beating of his heart.

At last the tips of fingers, the hands, arms, head of Don Carlos rose. But the Señor was in pain. He crawled out, and stretched himself in the arabesque of light and shade under the tree; panting, groaning, pressing pallid fingers on eyes which ached and throbbed.

The mayordomo clasped his own brown palms together and prayed: '*Madre de Dios, ruega por nosotros! Miserere Domine!*' A jumble of languages; a confusion of ideas, perhaps; but it came from the poor man's heart. A tear, too, came from his flashing eye.

Carlo lay groaning on the brink of despair; but turning and seeing one in prayer, he felt a little strength. Then they searched the ground for some distance round the poplar, wherever the hind legs of the bear had cast the litter about, hoping that a fragment of the gold chain might afford them some little clue, some thread of hope.

Carlo's heart sickened. He trembled like one of the leaves upon the trembling tree, when he clasped it round the trunk, and felt that all his hope, now as yesterday, was up among those silvery stems.

No, he could not let Cristóbal go up, though the *vaquéro's* heart was bold, and eye bright. The heart he prized, more than earth and heaven, hung in that bower. It had been intrusted to him. He must find, keep, and cherish it.

Up he went, sustained by a strong desire; with eager eyes, and delicate touch, examined all that he could reach; far out on branches where man had never lain before, drawing in the slender twigs, turning over every leaf; climbing higher, far higher than yesterday, straining his sight, to scan the very crown of sunlit leaves, and all in vain.

O man! Take heart. Is not love, love? Will an opal break the charm? Are not links of passion more durable than gold? No, no; there is a tumult in his ears, a murmur full of bitterness and woe: '*So mayest ever keep my heart.*'

Down he came recklessly, drawing blood from his fingers, tearing his clothes, crashing leaf and twig, without thought, without regard; and found William with Cristóbal, watching him gravely.

W. B. Well, Carlo; you can make nothing of it?

C. Nothing but heartache.

W. B. Too long under water, I dare say.

C. [Bitterly.] That's nothing, Will. You don't know——

He could get no farther; but bit his under-lip, so that the blood spurted out; while a deadly pallor spread over the rest of his face.

They took him to the great house at San Pedro, where a deep sleep fell upon him. Let us leave him there in charge of his old nurse, retrace our steps a little way, and see how William Briggs thought and acted upon this occasion.

When Carlo was wringing his shirt out, under the sycamore tree, after he had been rescued from that quaking poplar, William noticed the absence of a small gold chain which his friend had worn for many weeks.

' I suppose he leaves it at home sometimes,' thought William. ' A bad plan ! '

For this big Saxon, with a reflective habit of mind, and great energies, which he rather held in reserve than fretted with constant use, was not free from a tinge of superstition. ' A bad plan ! ' he repeated; ' I've known evil to come of it.'

You may remember that he was smoking, and gazing into the western sky. His eyes were fixed on the glories of the setting sun with that dead look which a man's eyes wear when his soul has gone back, back through the dreamy past, to some terrible hour when perhaps some calamity befel him, something which has made him other than he was.

You will remember also that he asked the other what he was thinking about up in the tree. His misgivings were confirmed on learning that Carlo in

that predicament had forgotten all about his love :
' For,' he thought, ' the girl was as much concerned
in the roots of that tree as he was.'

Then, as they rode to the boundary, he thought,
' He seems to have forgotten all about her. I don't
like his leaving that chain at home.' But when, later
in the evening, he again broached the subject, and
found that the chain bore an amulet, and that both
were lost, he roused himself, and said again, ' Evil
might come of this ; but I will hinder it. What
profits experience of ill, if not to see it coming, and
to wrestle with it ? '

So he questioned Carlo, and ascertained that the
chain was lost between midnight of the Vigil and
sunset of the Feast. Strange as it must seem, his
suspicion at once took wing over land and sea, and
pounced upon Don Marcos, at that time cruising in
the Californian Archipelago. We have no wish to
disparage the character of that hero, but William
Briggs was a superstitious and a curious fellow. He
mused in this way :

' He knows that Mariano has banished Carlo till
the Carnival, and that he is only to write once in the
interval. There is persistency of purpose in the
man. I saw the dogged look on his face, and the
twinkle in his eye. Gold may prosper where powder
and lead failed. Some such idea as that. ' Ay,
Marcos ; but there are metals with a truer ring than
gold.'

At first he thought that their two Indians must be

the agents. He dealt with them at once; but in neither did he see a trace of cunning, of suspicion, or reserve.

Then came the little talk with Angela, in private:

W. B. Tell me, *Commadre mia*; did anyone pass this way [indicating with his hand the passage from the Casa to San Pedro] on the night of the Vigil?

A. No, señor.

W. B. Nor that way? [indicating the contrary.]

A. No, señor.

W. B. Ni mañanito—Nor in the early morning?

A. No, señor.

W. B. Nor in the forenoon of the Feast?

A. Only Don Carlos.

But presently Thomasito let fall that, about the hour of Angelus, on the Vigil, Costinetto had passed from the Hacienda to Santa Perona, on the other side of the ford. Did Thomasito hail him? No: it was the hour of prayer: the boy was saying his '*Padre Nuestro.*' How was Costinetto mounted? On *el blanco*. [This was the white horse which Juanita used to ride; one noted for speed and endurance.]

The conversation passed on smoothly to other matters, but William soon afterwards, leaving Carlo and the mayordomo, rode round to the great house of the Buenaventuras.

'Costinetto was here on the Vigil?' he said to La Forina.

L. F. Si, señor.

W. B. Did he go to keep the Feast?

L. F. The *Señor* was there.   Did he not ?

W. B. I left at noon with Cristóbal.   I saw him not.

Then William went on to the *Ranchería*, and found that Don Pedro and the others had returned during the night, and were then sleeping in the dust, like lizards.   The Don was to bring a party over in the afternoon to renew their labours at the Casa Briggs. Costinetto had not been seen.   He had not kept the Feast.   Don Pedro observed that his kinsman was a Gentile and a *ladrone*, and so composed himself for a little more slumber.

But William returned to La Forina ; told her that the amulet was lost, and that he had bound himself to find it.   Could she help him ?   The old woman was frightened at the loss.   She must see Don Carlos.

And it has been related how she saw him, and was likely to see much of him for the next few days.

He started and twitched and groaned in his sleep, like a man in fear and in pain.   When he awoke, and saw her sitting on the foot of his bed, rocking herself to and fro, he said, ' O, my mother, is it thou ?   Hast been here all the time ? '

L. F. Three long hours, waiting to hear thy voice.

C. I have had that dreadful dream again.

L. F. Which dream ?

C. A shadow coming between me and the stars.

L. F. The shadow of a man ?

C. Yes ; an old man like Costinetto, with blood-shot eyes.

In the meanwhile William repaired to Don Pedro, told him that he was going on a journey, and must have *el blanco.* He should start an hour after sunset, wishing to travel all night. There appeared a per-plexity in William's plans here, for he had also instructed Cristóbal to have *el negro* in readiness for him at the same time.

The *Hacienda* was scoured far and near. The two *caballadas* were driven in, and corraled. The Señor might take horses and men : all were at the service of his Grace, but *el blanco* was missing.

Next, the Señor wanted an escort. He would have Costinetto, no other. A new *sarape* to man or boy would bring Costinetto, by an hour after sunset. How unreasonable was this *Inglés* ! Not an Indian head was wanting but that of the gambler, the Gentile, the *ladrone. Que carajo !* And no other would do.

Manuel and Francisco had nothing to tell. The house had been swept, the clothes hung out in the sun ; they had worked at their saw-pit, anxious as Don Guillermo could be to hasten the auspicious day and dollars.

So William gave directions how the work was to proceed in his absence, and rode back to bid his friend farewell. Carlo was still more than half asleep.

Day had given place to night again. Two or three women moved silently about the deserted corridors. William lingered for a moment in the gloom. ' In this populous world,' he thought, ' there must be some deserted houses, some passages which only echo with the memory of soft foot-falls, of words which once made music in the ear and heart.'

CHAPTER XXII.

FOUND.

—— An amulet, that keeps
Intelligence with you ;
Red when you love, and rosier red,
And when you love not, pale and blue.

THREE years before the date of these events, the
Señor Arianas, marking the great influx of popu-
lation to the north, concluded that a demand for
grapes would soon arise. So he set his gardens at
Los Angeles in order, engaging a Sonorian vine-
dresser, by name Don Gabriel.

A tribe of civilised Indians, calling themselves
' Aguas Calientes '* (Hot-waters), supplied labourers
for the vineyards ; and, during the grape harvest,
extra ' hands' of women and girls were levied from
the *Pueblo.*

Meanwhile a great distillery rose in San Francisco:
a company was also formed for making wine at Los
Angeles ; and the grapes of the Señor Don Mariano
Arianas, together with those of the Doña Julalia, his
cousin, commanded the markets. This year, thou-

* From some springs in the neighbouring mountains.

sands of cases, filled with plump Malagas, were sent
by sea to San Francisco ; and the production of a
large juicy lemon promised soon to become a mine of
wealth.

So the hidalgo and his family are passing the
autumn in this resort. I should like to draw you a
picture of Don Mariano's pretty villa, with its broad
shadowy balconies, in which you see doors and
windows, like dark openings to a lonely grot, through
a wall of climbing rose and jasmine. But you must
picture it to yourself. I can only hint that such
was their abode.

The house stands in a plot of thirty acres, enclosed
with a tall willow hedge. Twenty acres are devoted
to the Malaga grape ; but near the house is a grove
of lemon and orange trees, a tiny water-course, and
the never-failing fountain. The domain is called
' Las Rosas ;' an appropriate name ; for in this genial
climate roses are in blossom throughout the winter,
or rather through that delicious season which cor-
responds to our winter, but can only be compared to
an Andalusian May on the banks of the Guadal-
quivir.

Gaiety is not a prominent feature of the best
society in Mexican towns : and though the Pueblo de
Los Angeles, at the date of our story, belonged to the
United States, its social aspect remained unchanged.

Fandangos, and other merry-makings, are frequent
during the Carnival, and on the feast-days of favourite
saints ; but the upper class partake sparingly of

these festivities, and, indeed, affect a greater exclusiveness and gravity of demeanour in town than in the seclusion of their *Ranchos.*

If the society of Los Angeles was at all influenced by its political transfer, the effect was a more zealous retirement of the respectable class, and a bolder levity on the part of the disreputable : though this may be justly attributed to its position, at the end of a line of immigration from the old States, and to the temptations which it offered to persons of infamous character, who, on their way to the gold-region, would linger in the pretty *Pueblo,* leaving marks of lawlessness and vice behind them.

So the tall willow fences became taller, the wattled branches locked each other in more rigid bands. Nothing met the eye but walls of pale green leaves ; but, from within, odours of jasmine and orange filled the air, or a hum of voices might be heard where a group of women were gathering and packing grapes.

Through these suburbs of Los Angeles, the water of a mountain-stream is carried in an aqueduct, distributing little channels to irrigate these solitudes ; for at the back, that is on the eastern side, of the town, rise the bluffs of Temescal, above which looms the great Cerro of Saint Anthony.

But about the *Plaza,* in the more populous part of the town, through doorways which are doorless, through *ventanas* which are windowless, may be seen the hammock's gentle motion, with the impress of a human form, if it is the afternoon; no less than in the gilded cabin of the *Yegua Negra,* now riding at anchor in the roadstead of Saint Peter, whence, on a soft western gale, or in the quiet of the afternoon *siesta,* is borne the long murmur of the solemn wave.

At daybreak, on the 3rd of October, a packet steamed into the roads, fired a signal-gun, sent a passenger on board the yacht of Don Marcos, some bales and letter-bags on shore, and, steaming out to sea again, held on its way to San Diégo.

The letter-bag contained despatches for the Señor Don Mariano, but not a word of comfort for Juanita. And to judge by the manner of the others, little comfort had been conveyed to them through the medium of the *General Jackson.*

But let us return to Juanita. The reader will remember how a shadow fell upon the breakfast-table at San Pedro, on the morning of the 4th of August—a cold, grim shadow, that of death, who had stalked through the valley in the morning mist.

After an interval less sad than agreeable, the lady returned to Los Ojitos, as we saw in a former chapter. In her eyes the place looked desolate and barren; and, indeed, the great plain was of a uniform straw-colour, for the grasses had withered in the valleys, and oat-stubble lay prone upon the uplands. They

R

arrived by the light of such a moon as that which lit her first parting with Don Carlos ; a large silver moon, climbing slowly above the mountain-tops.

'Ah!' she thought, 'it is ever *Adios! adios!* Mockery of words ; for the heart clings to man. Poor heart, always torn and rent, and mocking itself with words in which no comfort lies !'

If the lady was unreasonable, I cannot help it. I don't undertake to draw an ideal heroine, but this poor *donzella,* as she was.

She did not mean that words are powerless to convey any kind of comfort : on the contrary, she seemed anxiously to desire some such, looking wistfully at every traveller who passed southwards, or who stayed to ask *posada* at the *Rancho.*

Wearily the month of August wore away. Time loiters with one who looks for that which comes not! All day, one longs for the night ; all night, sighs for the day ! Expectation closes round you like a dull dead mist. Out of the mist comes a voice which mutters something, lowly in an undertone, so that you become familiar with the sound, before the sense, of what it has to say.

Twice or three times Juanita strove with her unseen enemy. She sought to tell her mother what she was going through, but could not. To complain of him, to tell anyone that she wondered why he did not write, that such a long silence was more than she could bear, that she allowed herself to think strange things of him, to doubt him, seemed more difficult every day, became impossible. She wrapt herself in the dead mist; the voice whispered in her ear, and the poison crept into her heart.

But the mother noticed this trial of her child, and she, too, wondered why Don Carlos did not write. When they parted, it had not been decided whether he should return to England to settle his affairs. Surely he had not left without a word, without riding a few leagues out of his way, without leaving a letter at San Miguel!

Don Mariano did not observe these misgivings. His hands were full. He omitted to mention that he had consigned Don Carlos to a banishment of six months, and had restricted the number of letters. But Carlos supposed that they were in his confidence.

Passing through San Luiz on the 2nd of September, they were entertained by Don Bernardo. He had received a messenger from Santa Perona, with a letter in the writing of Don Guillermo. The letter contained no allusion to Don Carlos. Don Bernardo knew nothing of the *caballéro's* movements. So another little glimmer of hope died out, and the lady travelled southwards, by sea, to Los Angeles.

She had a rebellious heart; and it rose up in clamour, on the sixteenth of that month, when the *Jupiter* sent on shore mail-bags from the northern ports, and, after all those heart-aches, not a word of comfort came to her. 'My heart is breaking,' she said; 'I have loved in vain. Ah me! bitter, bitter woe! What a dreary world to live in!' But the house was a bower of roses; and in the orange-groves, hard by, Don Gabriel was humming a roundelay.

And as he hummed, the words of her thought formed a refrain to his song, 'In vain, in vain; I have loved in vain.'

So the mist which had swathed her drew back a little, still shutting out all beautiful and holy sights which lay around her, but giving place to pride, a wounded, angry spirit, which fluttered round, and goaded her heart into some such utterance as this: 'I threw myself at his feet, and he scorned me. I went to be near him; but he stayed away, or coming tardily, preferred another, and gave my token to a stranger. All this I forgave him; but why did he claim me? Why fold me to his heart, and mock me with kisses? Cruel and unkind!'

For wounded pride is spiteful, and bears false witness. It painted Carlo as a man of violence, who made a sport of love. Juanita looked upon the picture, and thought she recognised the lineaments.

And, looking on this false picture, she forgot the tender traits of nature, and knew not that she had forgotten them: coldness which melted in a woman's presence; the taming of *el pinto*; the last will and testament of Carlo, as he went on the war-trail in the pass of Chelone; those things which La Forina, and those which Angela, had told her; the self-imposed solitude and sadness in the Glade of Oaks; the long, eager gaze in the forest; the pistol fired in the air; the tender solicitude during her illness, and the like, she saw no longer. The picture wore another aspect.

So the month of September came and went; but Juanita was unconscious of the letter which Carlo had written, and of those subsequent events which took place on the little *Rancho*.

As the early days of October came over the Cerro of Saint Anthony, lingered in the sultry sky, and died on the margin of the sea, the angry spirit left her for a time, and the dull, dead mist of hope deferred closed round her. '*Mañana*,' she moaned, '*mañana, y nunco ser mañana,*—The morrow, the morrow, which comes, but never is!'

As the third day broke, she heard the signal-gun of a mail-boat. Wildly the blood coursed through her veins. Every pulse beat and throbbed tumultuously. Every sound from without made her start and quail as though some evil threatened her, as though she knew it coming, and suffered ere it came. At last it came. The letters were delivered; but to her, not a word of comfort.

Then, on the next day, came Alberto, with the basilisk eye, and quiet sneer. 'Poor *muchácha*! the Inglés loves thee. Be comforted! But the *caballéro* returns to his land. He has forgotten to say farewell! And thy little jewel, *la joyita*. [How she started! She seemed to have forgotten the amulet.] The *caballéro* keeps it not. It is nothing.'

The mist vanished. The angry spirit fled abashed. Up rose the true heart, in wrath. ' Coward!' she exclaimed, stamping her little foot, shaking back her glossy hair, and looking defiance into the basilisk eye. But the eye gleamed ominously, the lips parted in a smile, showing a double crescent of white teeth, as Alberto drew slowly from an inner pocket the coils of a golden cord, the amulet in its faded silk bag, which also contained a golden tress.

Handing these to his brother's child, Don Alberto languidly withdrew. But Nita sat down upon the greensward, and leaned her back against the rim of the marble basin, playing with her jewel listlessly; while the spray of the fountain danced about her, glistening, like dew-drops, on her hair, her dress, on her very hands, as she wound the golden loops about her fingers.

Unlike Nita, as she stood by another fountain, putting the chain round her lover's neck, in the quaint particoloured light of Chinese lamps!

But let us watch her for a moment. She unties the string of the little sachet, takes out the shining tress, and kisses it; lays it down, takes out the amulet sadly. But see! Her cheek brightens; she draws a long breath through parted lips, tears gush from her eyes, her face is hidden in her hands; down she bends, and the fountain casts its spray upon her drooping head, while her soft palms are watered with a flood of tears.

For, as she drew the opal from its case, a furtive sunbeam smote it; and at once the amulet glowed like a heart of fire: so Nita knew that her love was true.

Looking up after a time, she became aware of a tall figure, dusty and travel-stained, standing where Alberto had stood before.

'Who brought it?' he said, in a solemn tone.

'Alberto,' she answered.

'Is Don Marcos here?'

'There,' she said, pointing seawards.

'It came that way,' he continued.

Then she rose and clung to his arm, as the passion-flower clings to a giant palm.

'Go on,' she said.

'I traced it to Monterey. There I saw the steamer in the offing, and have ridden a hundred leagues to save you this pain, but am late.'

'No, no,' she said. 'Go on.'

'It was stolen from him, as he slept, on the Vigil of Saint Michael.'

Then Juanita leaned her fair brow on William's breast, sobbing and weeping passionately, with self-reproach; and Julia, hearing these sounds, drew near, and saw what was taking place.

When Don Guillermo saw her, he held out the hand which was disengaged without embarrassment; and the *Doña* came and greeted him.

'" *Buéna sea tu venida.*" Well is thy coming,' she

said, quite calmly. But five minutes before she had been thinking of him, at Santa Perona, far away, beyond the purple hills.

'*Tia*,' William said to her, with a smile. 'Give this to the *Señorita* by-and-by.' This was Carlo's letter, which William had brought from San Luiz Obispo, where it had missed the steamer, as he had done at Monterey.

CHAPTER XXIII.

MEETINGS BY MOONLIGHT.

THE last chapter closed with a scene which was enacted in the garden of Las Rosas.

As the family of Arianas and their guest sat in the Piazza that evening, apparently on good terms with each other, William said he had an adventure to relate. The ears of all were intent to hear. So he told it as follows:—

'Having kept the Vigil of Saint Michael at the Mission, Cristóbal and I, who had a wife and a friend at home, started after mass, on the feast day, and took the lower trail, that which leads to the boundary of the two estates.

'The country, as you must know, is arid at this season, being, after you emerge from the pass, little more than undulating sweeps of sand, or dusty stubble, yawning and gaping where the soil is firmest, as though crying out for a drop of water. Is it not so?' he said, turning to Juanita, who sat near him.

'I thought it beautiful as we came along,' she said. Poor innocent! The beauty was in her heart.

Fresh springs, green grasses, and the song of the turtle-dove, had all been there.

'Yes,' replied William, gravely; 'but you see the Feast of St. Michael occurs later in the season. The land was parched. When we were about two leagues from the boundary-lodge, we heard, on our right, thunder; yes, surely it was a peal of thunder: no—what then? A long low angry roar, which ceased for a moment now and then, breaking out again, more angrily and deeply. It was a *wounded bear at work*: at what work? We soon conjectured. Well Cristóbal knew the sound, having heard it once before.

'So we turned aside, and rode straight for the Agua Muerte: swiftly and more swiftly, into that dreaded circle of sound; nearer and nearer to the centre whence it came. The horses were bathed in foam. *El negro* was as white as——' but, turning to the Señorita, William saw she too was a deadly white.

'Well, the story will soon be ended, and all's well that ends well; but my poor horse was overweighted, and the mayordomo disappeared over a low round ridge, while we struggled on, *El castaño* and I.'

'Quick, señor,' gasped Nita.

'Yes; I urged him on furiously, riding more like Don Carlos than myself. The tops of three tall poplars rose above the ridge, one swaying to and fro terribly; at last the whole trees, and between me and them, Cristóbal, making a cast.'

' For the love of the blessed Virgin, quick !' whispered Nita, drawing close.

' From the base of the tree which rocked came a smothered groan, instead of the loud roar. *El negro* had turned, and was struggling fearfully, to loud cries of the mayordomo, for the bear was immoveable, clutching——'

' A-a-ah ! Quick, for the love of God !'

'—— clutching the strong roots, immoveably ; so I dismounted, and shot him through the head.'

' And——?' they all asked in a breath.

' Yes ; I was forgetting : Don Carlos descended from the tree.'

' *Libre de daño ?*'

' Unhurt.'

' *Ave Maria santissima !*'

' But on the next day, what with grief and vexation at his loss, what with staying too long under water diving for an opal, climbing bareheaded in the heat of noon looking for I wonder what, he fell ill, and we took him to La Forina, at San Pedro.'

Juanita took William's brawny hand in hers, raised and kissed it with simple fervour ; but he said, ' I have earned no thanks ; they are due to our good Cristóbal.'

Then William, rising, stood by the side of Mariano, who was leaning against a rose-twined column, in his favourite attitude, with folded arms, and one leg across the other. ' Yours is a generous race,' said the Englishman ; ' you love to thank when little has been done, to give when nothing has been desired.'

We must bear in mind that William had been 'M. le Diplomate;' but, being an honest fellow, and withal a reflective one, he added, 'You grant a favour less readily when asked.'

'Julia felt a sharp pang, and gave a sudden start; but it passed unnoticed, for the two wax candles were far back in the dim *Estrado*, and our friends were sitting or standing in deep shade.

Don Mar. What favour, señor?

W. B. But we are a race who love not to ask.

Don Mar. I and my house are at your service; ask!

W. B. No; it was a passing thought. We have ample proofs of your kindness. Yet my friend would write more often to the Señorita.

Don Mar. Let him write, or let him come; Las Rosas is the home of Don Carlos.

Juanita then knew for the first time that Carlo had been withheld from writing. She had read his one letter, had forgotten two months of misery, or only remembered how she had wronged him, and having no place for an angry thought, said meekly, '*Gracias, señor.*'

And when the ladies had retired, Don Guillermo lingered in the piazza; but Don Mariano, having squeezed the juice of a lemon into a glass, filled it up with wine, and drank; then he paced the broad walks to and fro, revolving many things in his mind.

Fortune had lately dealt him two severe buffets.

The news had reached him by the mail which arrived that morning. The 'Agua Fria' bubble had burst, and with it had passed away $100,000, his whole realised property. The commissioners of inquiry into Mexican title-deeds had decided against his claim to the estate of Los Ojitos. So that the Señor Don Mariano was no longer rich.

And as he paced to and fro in the solemn stillness, a voice reached him from afar, a voice which spoke of something constant and enduring, of something strong to do and to bear. All through life it had sounded in his ears. When he had been alone, thinking good, or thinking evil—when every other voice was mute, he seemed to be not alone. That solemn murmur never ceased.

In youth it had spoken to him, and in middle age; in longing and regret; in joy and sadness; on his *Rancho*, or in the *Pueblo*; at rest, or on the road; and now it moaned reproachfully.

'Those girls!' he thought; 'I should have done it before this blow fell. Now I am poor. I am *vaquéro*, *Indio*! Not a rood of land, not a *fanéga* of barley, not a dollar, not one. *Jésu Cristo!*'

And still he heard the distant moaning of the wave.

'And my poor Juana! Sweet wife, so uncomplaining! And Marcos! Is the man ruined too? He must have heard this morning. I shall see him. Ah! no: he avoids me: thinks I shall upbraid him: Marcos, the son of our dear Renáldo!

'But those poor orphans! Is it their fault that my father begat them? Have they sinned? I thought the great *Inglés* loved the Rosebud, too. He might have taken her, if I had given her but a few dollars; ten thousand, even five: it is nothing. But now! [The Señor fixed his eyes upon the moon, which somehow appeared to him melancholy, that night.] Now my poor sisters will go singly, like the single moon.'

Having arrived at the end of a broad walk, the Señor turned his back upon the lonely moon; when, to his surprise, there met him a lady in a long white robe, with no mantle but a shower of brown hair, which fell round her shoulders.

These midnight meetings are terrible. The hidalgo started back, aghast.

'Be not angry with me, dear brother.'

'Ah! *hermanita,* is it thou?'

'It is I. [Julia.] I know of thy sorrow.'

No answer.

'Hast lost thy Rancho!'

Still no answer.

'The Agua Fria mine has stopped!'

A groan.

'Art well-nigh ruined, brother mine. Hast no money left. Canst not buy back thy Rancho!'

Another groan.

'But 'tis bought. 'Tis mine. I give it thee, dear brother. See here!'

And she handed him a paper.

Accumulated astonishment overpowered the stout hidalgo:

'*Ca—a—ramba!*' he exclaimed with emphasis, reading the paper by the light of the lonely moon.

She was right. It was the copy of a document purporting to resign the claim of the Superior and Holy Order of San Francisco to the *Hacienda* of 'Los Ojitos,' in consideration of certain moneys, not specified, paid over by Don Bernardo of San Luiz Obispo, on behalf of some person not specified.

'*CA-A-RAMBA!*'

Then Don Mariano, who, as the ladies thought, had been growing more reserved in manner, and more troubled about affairs, during the last three years, took Julia in his arms, and kissed her, saying, 'Go thou to bed, my pretty Rose. Hast taught me to be generous.'

The Rose vanished among the roses, and the Señor stood wondering. 'Who has done this? Who has seen this impending evil, and gone before it with a remedy? Is it hidden from me? My dear brother, my José, my Joaquin!'

How came the Doña Julia by this important document? Don Guillermo, as we have seen, lingered in the Piazza when the ladies retired to rest. But as they went, he pressed the hand of Julia, and whispered one word, 'Return.'

And as he lingered, she appeared at his side, clad in white, and veiled in nature's mantle. ''At the service of your Grace,' she said, smiling.

'No,' he said, looking at her half sadly, 'not mine. Another needs it more than I.'

'What other?'

Then he told her of the two great losses which had befallen Mariano. 'But a friend, an old and tried friend,' he added, 'foresaw this calamity, and bought the claim of the Franciscans to Los Ojitos. Here it is. I am commissioned to give it you. You are ——' [Here William hesitated a moment, as if he had forgotten his instructions.] 'Yes, you are to do with it absolutely as you wish.'

Her hands trembled with the strange gift. 'Who is the giver?' she asked.

'An old friend, and one who will not miss the price of it,' he answered. '*Vaya, con Dios!*'

And she went.

The next morning, at break of day, Don Mariano and the Englishman stood upon the sea-shore, hailing a yacht in the roadstead. A strange story about the amulet had come to the hidalgo's ears. Strange thoughts about Don Marcos caused a tumult in his brain.

No response came from the schooner, which rode gracefully at anchor, swaying her bright masts against the horizon, and bowing to the surging sea. Again and again they hailed, but hailed in vain. The schooner slipt her cable; a gentle land-breeze caught the jib; round veered her head towards the south; the large mainsail slowly rose; and in a few minutes the *Black Mare*, under a press of white canvas, was gliding calmly away on the surface of the deep.

'It is strange!' said the Señor.

'Very,' answered William, whose keen eye was fixed on the stern cabin windows of the yacht. His companion, looking in the same direction, could just discern the wave of a long moustache under the brass rim of a spy-glass. Certainly that was the magnificent moustache of Don Marcos.

An hour afterwards Don Guillermo took his leave of the ladies. Having wished the others *Adios*! and having Doña Julia's hand in his, William said, 'The other, too.' So she gave him the other; two soft warm little hands. He lifted them up, looked at them, as if he expected to see some mark or sign upon them, and not seeing any such mark or sign, resigned them, with half a sigh.

How very curious of Don Guillermo! What strange persons are these *Ingléses*! A strange farewell, indeed! And he rode away.

CHAPTER XXIV.

OMNES EODEM COGIMUR.

Why lingereth she to clothe her heart with love,
Delaying; as the tender ash delays
To clothe herself, when all the woods are green?

WE shall hurry over the events of the next few
months. Towards the end of November, the
Señor Don Mariano, with wife and child and sisters,
returned to Los Ojitos.

In those days Julia grew sadder and sadder. No
murmur passed her lips: still she had a quiet smile
for those who greeted her : but the eyelid ever
drooped: the rosy bloom of health left her cheek;
and its mantling was with a hectic flush which came
and went. She would sit much alone with Francesca,
her sister, and sing little songs which they had learnt
in childhood. Once they were vague melodies which
hovered about creations of the fancy, or spoke of an
abstract sentiment. Now a strange new meaning
gave them force. She was learning to speak the
heart-language from her heart. One of these *cancions*
ran thus: It is by Cristóbal de Castilléjo, the last of
the Romancéros.

> El me quiere más que así;
>> Yo le mato de cruél;
>> Mas, en ser lo contra el,
> Tambien lo soy contra mí:
> De ver-le penar así,
>> Muy penada vivo yo;
>> Y remedio no le do!

> More than little he loves me;
>> Cruel am I, and yet a tear
>> Dims my loving eye, for fear
> I kill him with cruëlty:
> Still I suffer more than he,
>> Seeing that he suffers so;
>> Shall I own it? No, ah no!

Another favourite of Julia's, at that time, may be rendered as follows:—

> I know not what this phantom is, which wanders
>> About the brain.
> My lone heart knoweth not: yet darkly ponders
>> Upon its pain.
>
> I hear the sad sea moaning round the bases
>> Of the lone hills:
> Sad as the sea, sad memory embraces
>> Wide tract of ills:
>
> Dim hopes which glimmer, like to distant mountains,
>> In fading light,
> Through tears which flow, like never-failing fountains,
>> By day and night.

Juanita sought to gain her confidence. One day, as Julia was leaving her room in the upper corridor, Nita met her, and taking Julia's arm drew it round her waist.

It was the hour of noon. The great ocean stretched away before them in a boundless expanse of sunlight. Autumn grasses clothed the land to its very brink. But below them lay the *Ramada*, and, on one side, the log of pine for fire-wood, with the ready axe.

It recalled to each an old scene, a scene of the early spring ; but the months which had intervened were ages—cycles through which the heart had orbed, in rain and sunshine, in darkness and in light.

The axe lay still. The log was at rest. But fancy painted the English stranger, *El güero grande*, poising the bright blade in the sunlight, and ringing down sharp frequent blows on the startled wood, which flew to right and left in glistening wedges.

' *Gentil hombre, bien criado,*' said Juanita, in a low voice ; ' hast forgotten, Julia ?'

' No, sweetheart.'

' Saidest then, that he was kind and brave ? Wert right, love ; he is also true.'

' True :' and Julia sighed : for she knew too well that William was kind and true.

' Tell me thy secret, love,' whispered the fair tempter.

But Julia leant her face on Juanita's shoulder ; and the latter could feel the hot tears in her breast, as Julia murmured, ' 'Twill kill me as it is. Ask me no more.'

Madre talked to her lord about this sadness which

had taken possession of Julia. 'She has no dower,' said the hidalgo: 'is she not dear to us? Let her take a thousand cows.'

It was a princely dower. An Arianas was not to be outdone in generosity. 'Francesca, too, shall be cared for,' Madre said; 'am I not her mother?' But still Julia grew paler and more languid every day.

When alone in their chamber, Francesca would say to her,

'Art brave, my sister? Hast courage to be true, to tell him all?'

But Julia said, 'The time is past. I should have told him long since. Now he loves an Arianas: but who am I? Cruel fate!'

Francesca. I think 'tis thee whom he loves; not thy father, or thy mother, or any name.

Julia. Is he not *caballéro de su tierra?*'

Francesca. Is he not generous?

Again Julia sighed. Hope had not died out, but struggled faintly with despair.

And in dreamy moments, the airy castles of her fancy's building were humble bowers. 'Alas! would God he were still the poor *Gambusino,* and no *caballéro!* Then fair would be my lot. Then this taint would be no bar between us. My love would fold me in his arms, and I should feel the beating of that loyal heart: Ah! blessed vision, stay!'

But it vanished, as such frail figments will do, and

the Señor Don Guillermo seemed to recoil from her with loathing: for when love is thrown back upon the heart, will it still be love?

Then came the Señor Don José. He had been spending a few days at the *Hacienda*, and came over to visit his sister before returning to the capital.

He condoled with his brother-in-law concerning that *desdichada*, the Agua Fria Mining Company. The name of Don Marcos was barely mentioned; for the subject was a sore one. That speculator had sold out his shares, at par, before the catastrophe occurred. Why should he have neglected to warn his father's friend?

A more serious charge stood against him. Don Guillermo had traced Costinetto on *El blanco* to Monterey. The captain of the steam-ship *General Jackson* had sent such a passenger on board the *Yegua Negra*, in the roadstead of Los Angeles. Don Alberto, who brought the amulet to Juanita, and made the false charge against Don Carlos, had sailed in the yacht with Don Marcos. Nor had Costinetto returned. These things looked very like the salient points of a defeated conspiracy.

Don Mariano naturally supposed, as did the others at Los Ojitos, that the 'old and tried friend,' of whom William had assured Julia that he 'would not miss the cost' of that document which restored Los Ojitos to its lord, could be none other than the Señor Don José.

From the day and hour when he and Mariano

had crossed swords, *calidâ juventâ*, he had been their friend, though secretly, for many years, from a feeling of filial respect. That powerful roan horse, which the stout Mariano ever rode, had been bred beyond Las Salinas. Messengers would come to Los Ojitos, and go silently, as they came, but ever leaving some token of a brother's love—a trifle, perhaps, in itself, in the eyes of Madre or her husband, a gem of price.

Now Mariano thought he would sound his brother, and see if he would acknowledge this crowning act of friendship, and receive those thanks which were his due.

Mar. 'Twas a terrible loss; a hundred thousand piastres!

José. Sad indeed, brother; but thy cattle are worth tenfold their ancient price.

Mar. True. But I lost more than gold.

José. How?

Mar. The commissioners decided in favour of the monks.

José. Ca-Ramba!

Mar. I lost my *Rancho.*

José. Valga-me Dios!

Mar. But, walking in my garden of Las Rosas, by the light of a lovely moon, there came to me a sweet maiden with the title in her hand, saying, 'Dear brother, I give it thee.'

José. Ave Maria!

Mar. 'Twas the Rosebud. [So he was wont to call Julia.]

José. A sweet flower, indeed.

Mar. A bounteous flower.

José. And the maid is dowerless?

Mar. A thousand cows. *Es nada.*

José. Buéno, mi hermano! But how came she by the document?

Astute hidalgo! He would not part with his little mystery on such easy terms. But in the afternoon, being alone with Julia, he took her hand, and looking at her significantly, said,

'Wert happy at San Pedro, *hermanita*?'

'I was happy,' she answered, gently.

'The place will be sad enough without thee.'

Julia did not look up, but felt that an earnest gaze was fixed upon her sad face. And a nameless dread seized upon her. 'Why gave he the title to me, and not to Mariano?' she thought. O cruel fate! The Señor Don José loved her. She had sold herself to him.

Voices drew near. Some welcome interruption was at hand. But no; the sounds passed away: again she was left with her friend, and her fear.

He went on relentlessly: 'Art thankless, *hermanita*?'

The thermometer in the corridor stood at ninety degrees; but Julia's gratitude was at zero.

'I am not thankless, señor,' she said, belying her heart.

'There are no flowers in my gardens of San Pedro.'

'None.'

'Wilt come and bloom there?'

'*Santa Maria!*' she thought; 'let me die!'

Then she fell back upon her own heart, thinking to find death lurking there. But she found courage, and so spoke out, and told the Señor, bravely, a dreadful secret, which none knew save her sister Francesca and Don Mariano.

The Señor drew back in amazement: '*Valga-me Dios!*' he exclaimed—this time in earnest; for he was shocked and surprised.

After a little while he regained his composure. 'Poor child,' he groaned, 'frail flower! Has been planted on a desolate shore! Yet take courage. The man hath a noble soul, and is loyal to himself.'

It was Julia's turn to start: 'What man? Quick! Speak!'

'Don Guillermo, sister mine; wouldst have another? My good friend and mayordomo, hath he not loved thee?'

Ah! that was music from the spheres! And in fact William had assented to the Señor's request that he should reside at San Pedro, and superintend the estate.

'But the man is poor,' continued Don José.

'How, poor?'

'Land, cattle, silver; all are gone.'

'Thanks to God! I have a dower. How came he poor?'

'Hast not guessed, simple one?'

' Guessed ? '

' 'Twas his gift he gave thee ; his all : I knew it not.'

' Mother of God ! I thank thee.'

And Julia sat still, and wept and prayed. Don José rose and left her. She saw him not. Her heart and soul and eyes were full to overflowing.

The sagacious reader has anticipated this little disclosure, doubtless.

When William rode to Monterey in quest of the amulet, startling intelligence reached him. Thence he rode post-haste to San Luiz, and called upon Don Bernardo. That merchant, knowing that the title to Los Ojitos would revert to the Franciscan monks if Don Mariano failed to satisfy the commissioners, had speculated. He had bought the contingency of the monks.

Underrating its value, or anxious to serve an old friend and client, he instructed William to offer the contingency to Mariano for $12,000. William considered $10,000 a fairer sum. They discussed the difference, and finally agreed to divide it. William closed at once, to the astonishment of Don Bernardo, who pocketed William's order on Messrs. Davidson and May for $11,000.

But poor William rode away with a certain document in his pocket, and nothing more ; for in giving that fatal order to the merchant he had overdrawn his account by some $500.

Now the Doña Julia was haunted by the words of Don José, ' The man hath a noble soul, and is loyal to himself.' Truly. But to love her, who had gained his love in a false guise : would not his loyal heart shrink from such a juggle ?

At least, she had not sought to gain his love. There was comfort in that thought. 'The just man will do me justice. He will pity me ; and pity is akin to love.'

Sometimes she would cry out against the injustice of her lot. Then feeling that a wisdom above her ken had decreed it, she prayed for grace to bear it; and again comfort came to her.

In the meanwhile Don Guillermo had returned to the little *rancho*. The new *casa* was finished. Don Carlos was now here, now there. His movements were no longer restricted. The Señor Don José, coming down to his estate, again urged William to come and reside there, as his mayordomo.

From sundry hints which the hidalgo let fall, William fancied that before long a young wife would come to reign supreme at San Pedro. His suspicions rested on Clem. What more probable ? Indeed, he had seen, or thought he had seen, the partiality with which Don José regarded his little friend.

But now the talk was all of Los Ojitos. Clem was never alluded to. Julia, or hints which implied something concerning that lady, fell from the hidalgo's lips. Could it be ?

The more William thought of it, the less improbable it seemed. Julia's evident wish to discourage

William's suit deepened his impression that she had given her heart to another. When he told her that it was an old and tried friend who had intrusted him with a document for her, how gladly she took it! He had played into his rival's hands. She loved him, and to bring this about the prudent man had ruined himself.

And now he must go there and live as this man's bailiff, and see her happy. 'Could I bear it?' he asked of himself. 'What? not endure that she should have nought to endure; not bear to see her happy?'

So he consented to the proposal of Don José.

One thing William had decided on long ago. Experience had led him to the resolve, that neither joy nor grief should have it their own way with him. 'So long as I am master, let it stay,' he thought: 'if it be joy, so; if grief, why so. One gets good out of either.'

But when the Señor was gone, William's heart spoke out plainly. This trial would be more than he could bear. The very prospect was madness.

Once more he took his friend into council; and this time the other did not administer to him bitter pills, but sweet.

C. You have bound my tongue for five months, Will; but now I tell you, as before, the girl loves you, and no other. If she marries another, thereafter say 'Mea culpa.'

W. B. The proof?

C. A hundred signs. Do you remember saying that you preferred a natural wreath? [William nodded.] Well, I have never seen her without one since. It is a sprig of willow now. [And William remembered that, on his visit to Los Angeles, it had been a spray of jasmine.] When I speak of you, she is all agog; or if she finds that we have been talking about ' *ellos por dentro* ' in her absence, she will take Juanita's hand, and fondle it, and say, ' What was it, Niña? ' [A long pause.] I'll tell you another thing which happened, the last time I was over there. Madre said, ' Will Don Guillermo never come again? ' and I was hypocrite enough to say, ' I fear not.' Julia was sitting back in the shade, but I saw her start, as she often does now, and another little sign I know; so I went to her and said, ' Give me one word, then.' But all she said was ' No, no; ' which I take to mean ' Yes ; ' and if I were you, I'd go.

W. B. Will you come with me ?

And their two hands closed, as the strength of one : while the eyes of each sought the other's heart, and found it full of manly love.

Here it is worthy of our notice that a thought of ' ways and means ' never came between William and his object. He was absolutely without property, unless a few cows and a brood-mare or two, with sundry bushels of maize or barley, could be raised to that rank. Nor did he dream of Julia's magnificent dower.

Happy man! who valued love more than gold, and

trusted to his strong arm and stout heart for all that
'life needs for life.'

The days of January are warm in that latitude :
but when the sun sets, a cold wind from the north-
west sweeps down the coast.

The 'family circle' were assembled in the Estrado,
at Los Ojitos, with closed doors, and a bright wood
fire on the hearth.   The Señores Don José and Don
Mariano were playing chess, with a celebrated set of
Chinese ivories which had been presented to the latter
gentleman in the spring of the former year.   Don
Estéban was thrumming on a guitar, now and again
trolling out the verse of a song, anxious for the dull
game to be ended ; but Madre watched the mimic
war with interest.

The three younger ladies were sitting at work :
but Juanita had left a skein of silk up-stairs.   'The
night is cold,' she said ; 'I wish Don Carlos would
return—and bring his friend,' she added, turning a
little, to look at Julia.   But Julia had left the room
noiselessly, to seek the skein of silk.

As the Doña sped along the corridor, the moon
peered through a drifting mist ; and in its uncertain
light she came upon a tall figure, leaning against a
column. She started back as if she had seen a ghost.

'*JULIA !*'

At that well-remembered voice she drew near and
extended her hand. How her heart palpitated ! 'Pass
in, señor,' she quavered, scarce knowing what she said.

'No : 'tis better so.' And turning his broad back to the wind, William sheltered her.

'Art cold and wet,' she pleaded; dropping the *usted* and the proprieties, in her agitation.

'It matters not, if thou art warm.'

He drew her nearer. She nestled in his breast, like a fledgling, in perfect simple trust. The man was so noble and true : what could she do less ?

'Forgive me ! forgive me !' she sobbed. 'Dear friend—great heart and true : I have let thee love me, and am unworthy of thy love.'

'How art thou unworthy ?' he asked, holding her off a little.

Her eyes flashed, and her cheek flushed, in that searching gaze.

'I dare not speak,' she said.

'Speak out, love—be the truth never so bitter. Art forgiven long before.'

'I am not what I seem.'

A shudder went through the strong frame of William. Perhaps it was the blast of the north-west wind. Yet he stood firm. 'What then ?' he asked.

'My father sinned.'

'Take courage, sweetheart !'

'My mother was a Pueblo girl.' And she covered her face with her hands.

But William drew her to his side again. 'Love is love,' he murmured in her ear; 'thy father's sin is nought to me. Let us thank God we are pure.'

And William's heart was relieved of a mighty load :

for Julia's manner had been so agitated, and her distress so great, that he feared some disclosure more terrible than this.

Her tears were flowing so fast now that she could not see him. The mists fled—the moon shone out brightly: but she wept and wept, till all memory of doubt, distrust, and sorrow had passed away, and left her abiding in the strong arms of love, then and for ever.

And now my tale is well-nigh ended. William's first suspicions concerning the probability of an alliance between Clem and the Señor Don José were better founded than those which usurped their place. That lady now reigns supreme at San Pedro, where probably the cares of a rising generation have tended to impair her epistolary powers.

Long after her union to the lord of San Pedro, and two other alliances which took place at the same time, the Doña Clem discovered that the little amber cross had come into her possession by very tortuous advances. She therefore returned it to the rightful owner, who thus ascertained that Don Carlos had not perpetrated the infidelity for which she had given him credit, and forgiven him more than once.

The thousand cows which Doña Julia had for her dower were deported across that ridge of the Coast Range known as Las Salinas; and to the present day goodly herds may be seen roaming the pastures between those mountains and the Sierra del Monte Diablo, marked with the brand **MB**.

Costinetto, the Gentile, did not return to San Pedro, but is supposed to be passing his declining years on the estate of San Blas, in Sonora. The proprietor of that domain has consoled himself for the loss of his intended bride : and Don Carlos has forgiven Don Alberto his complicity with that cavalier. When one is prosperous, it is so easy to forgive.

Don Bernardo, the merchant, on the other hand, has never been so cordial with his countryman, since William drove such a hard bargain with him for the contingent title to Los Ojitos. He expresses himself as rejoiced that the estate should have reverted to that arch-heretic Don Mariano Arianas. But to steal a march upon a fellow-countryman is unpardonable.

Lastly, the amulet is still worn by Don Carlos. That romantic person has quite convinced himself of its miraculous properties, and consults it, and seeks the aid of the venerable La Forina, on many interesting occasions.

LONDON

PRINTED BY SPOTTISWOODE AND CO.

NEW-STREET SQUARE

www.ingramcontent.com/pod-product-compliance
Lightning Source LLC
Chambersburg PA
CBHW021047030726
47496CB00006B/1721